# Miss Mezzanine

## MIKE SMITH

Rami,

From one writer to another, you are an inspirational. Thank you for all that you've done with this book.

*[signature]*

To Allison, for finding Miss Mezzanine's voice.
And to Alexa, for giving her one.

1

When I first heard the light sound of thunder from the car, I could only sigh in disappointment. Rain was sure to follow. I stuck my head out the passenger seat window to get a clearer look at the sky, and noticed overhanging clouds that had no looks of retreating. We were stuck in dead traffic a few hundred yards before the festival's entrance, and people all around us were beeping their horns. I shook my head in annoyance and rolled up the window. As the sounds of the horns faded, the indie rock music playing on our car radio reemerged. I turned it up a few notches just to drown out the noise pollution outside.

I turned to Greg; he appeared indifferent to the entire experience. Or maybe just bored. This didn't bother me; I imagined that my friend and roommate wouldn't have chosen to spend one of his last free weekends of our senior year watching indie artists perform at Portland's annual Konacks Festival. Instead, he was more the sports junkie, content to watch any football, basketball or hockey game from the comfort of his own home. But since I had committed to flying across the country to spend my last spring break in his hometown, my guess is that he felt obligated to entertain his houseguest. And though my knowledge of the Portland music scene was non-existent, my inclination for indie music over other genres was undeniable. So he bought us each a ticket to Konacks, essentially *Woodstock*-lite, complete with swarms of people wearing muddy sweatshirts that boasted their current place of enrollment, smoking weed or getting drunk in the parking lot.

We arrived at the concert, which in reality was just a giant field situated beside a Wal-Mart-sized parking lot. The lot was nearly full, but Greg managed to clinch a spot near the front in between two enormous vans. He put the car in park, but when I reached for the door handle, he motioned for me to stop. Then, he reached into his pocket and pulled out two joints.

"I saved these for a special occasion," he said, and passed me one.

I hesitated at first, staring at the joint as though it were some sort of foreign auto part. Neither Greg nor I were much for recreational drug use, only smoking the occasional bowl within the confines of a college dormitory, where the worst that could happen was getting your hand slapped by an RA. I wasn't a fan of smoking in public, always afraid that there would be a swarm of DEA agents just around the bend, waiting to pounce the moment we took our first puff. Even just looking at the weed in such an exposed space prompted me to scope the perimeter to make sure no one was watching. Still, for the sake of camaraderie, I pushed aside my paranoia and lit the joint.

Despite being sandwiched in between the vans, completely obscured from anyone's line of vision, I still leaned down as I took my first hit, trying to remain unnoticed. Doing so meant I was effectively blowing the smoke back into my own face, and so my initial coughing only resulted in more smoke entering my system. By the second hit, my eyes began to water. I handed the joint back to Greg, already entrenched in a fog of marijuana fumes. I suddenly couldn't help but laugh at how unnecessary it was to contort myself, seeing as how my figure was likely concealed within the car full of smoke.

Our time in the car only lasted a couple minutes; I took four hits and let Greg finish the rest. Was I high? Maybe. It was hard to tell, since I hadn't smoked in months. My sliding scale of intoxication that had begun when I was a freshman now tipped almost entirely toward alcohol, since drinking legally in public was much easier than smoking in private. Still, the pot had clearly mellowed me out; the noises and conversations surrounding me instantly muted, and for a brief moment I heard nothing but the sound of a guitar in the distance.

We exited the car and stretched our legs; between the long car ride and the smoking, mine felt like Jell-O. It was at least an hour before sunset, but the sky was getting darker. A cool misty rain had already begun, but no one seemed to notice. Nor did anyone seem prepared. I didn't spot one umbrella, jacket, or hat among the crowd. Not that I had much room to compare; I stood wearing just a t-shirt and jeans. The rain hitting my skin added to my high, as the consistent and soft touch of water coincided with my relaxed mood. As long as there was no pounding thunderstorm on the horizon, I was content.

Greg led the way into the concert. It was an odd venue: the parking lot ran right up against the edge of the field, where ten attendants were standing to collect tickets and 'let us in.' Music was already playing at the main stage, and there were three smaller stages set up farther down the field. We walked down the sloped grass toward the main stage—the only one with a cover extending from the front. A few hundred people had already gathered there, some standing and moving about, but most lounging on blankets and chairs in the grass. The band onstage consisted of four musicians, three of whom looked like they had just awoken from a long nap. The only one who appeared attentive was the violin player, who danced around the stage as she played her set. Her fast movements were what caught my eye, but the sound of the music was what ultimately caused me to stop walking and give her my full attention.

"Look at her," I said, tugging Greg's arm and pointing to the violinist. "Can you see the passion in her movements? She's adding percussion to the song by jumping around on stage. So intense."

"I think you smoked too much ganj," he responded. "It's just some chick prancing around the stage. Plus, she's hideous."

She wasn't very attractive; her hair was a faded red, and the extreme paleness of her skin looked borderline unhealthy. But each chord she played was harmonic and full of emotion, drowning out the keyboardist, drummer, and guitarist, whose lax approaches to their music didn't impress me much. Toward the end, the violinist sped up her play even more, hitting the pulse-pounding coda of their song and bouncing around the stage from one end to the other with an incredible fervor. I stood there, transfixed. After the song's last note, I burst into applause before anyone else in the crowd.

"Great song!" I screamed. I turned to Greg, who clearly wasn't impressed.

"Food?" he asked.

"Sure," I still said, my brief high fading and turning into hunger at the first mention of food. Apparently everyone else had the same idea, since the one concession stand I could see was packed with people, mostly our age. And judging by the smell, Greg and I apparently weren't the only ones who had indulged in weed. As we walked to the back of the line, I could already start to smell the grease wafting from the open window, promising the kind of high-caloric, heart attack-inducing slop that could only be found at outdoor concerts. A future stomachache was unavoidable, but at this point, I was willing to take that chance, and so I tried my best to block out the increasingly unpleasant scent.

"Beckett!" someone screamed. Greg and I turned around to find two guys standing behind us. They both looked like stereotypical stoners, sporting corduroy shorts and skateboarding t-shirts. Their bloodshot eyes and strong marijuana smell solidified my initial impression. The two guys exchanged a series of complicated hand gestures with Greg, the sort I recalled seeing back in junior high school. Greg pointed to me.

"Guys, this is Jass, my roommate at Tundra. Jass, this is Brock and Dom. We went to high school together. What are you guys doing out here?"

"Ah, you know, missed Konacks last year 'cause it was too cold. Didn't want to make any excuses this time." Brock pointed to the stage nearby. "You guys want to come hang? There's like five of us just chillin' over by the main stage."

I could tell Greg wanted to; he almost nodded yes before the guy finished making his offer. I didn't blame him, either; I knew his high would eventually wear off, and based on his reaction to the one set we had heard earlier, the music here had little to offer him. Plus, these guys probably had more pot.

"You all go ahead," I injected. "I'm going to scope the place out a bit. Get a feel for some of the other stages." The smell of the concession stand food intensified, and my earlier pangs of hunger were morphing into nausea. I needed to get out of there, and I didn't mind branching out on my own. Plus, I knew Greg would feel much more at ease tagging along with his old buddies if I was proactive about splitting up. As soon as Greg nodded, I hurried out of line. I didn't know quite where I wanted to go, but I definitely didn't want to stand there any longer.

I returned to the main stage, where the same band was

performing a slower song this time. The violinist sat this one out, drinking a bottle of water with her violin resting on her lap. Without the strings, the song had little to offer, so I ventured off to investigate the other bands. The lawn was like a minefield; I had to carefully navigate each step to avoid landing on someone's head. Gradually, I worked my way down the hill to the second stage. This one had no cover and held a much smaller crowd.

One man stood onstage playing a mandolin and singing just a hair faster than the chords he was strumming. Like the violinist, he played more than just the instrument, pounding his feet on the ground along with the beat. The other fifty or so people clustered at the front of the stage stood transfixed, eyes closed, swaying to the tune.

"You should cut him some slack. This is his first live gig."

I turned around but didn't see anyone at first. Then I saw a little hand and followed it down an arm to find a woman stretched out on a bright red blanket on the ground. Her smile caught me first, followed by her legs kicking in the air, her petite frame swaying back and forth. I had already seen about a hundred girls like her in the few minutes since I had arrived, but this one struck me as the best-looking and most energetic. From her clear eyes, I could also see that she wasn't high. Her smile instantly drowned out the sound of the mandolin behind me, and I could only smile back. She stopped kicking, and her smile faded. She brushed her flimsy bangs away from her face.

"I'm sorry," she muttered, "you just looked . . . I don't know. Unsatisfied." She laughed, but just enough to gauge my reaction. I shook my head, jerking my thumb at the stage.

"No, not at all." I laughed the same as she had, short and awkward. "I actually have no idea who that is. I'm new here."

"Well, first timer, you are in for a treat. His name is

Donegal, and he's one of the more underrated performers at this concert. His first album was a critical darling, but it didn't sell a ton of copies. And you know what the main perk of that is?"

I shrugged.

"Audience members are always guaranteed a good spot."

She pushed aside a water bottle and motioned for me to sit down. I didn't hesitate. Why was this girl sitting by herself anyway? I extended my hand.

"I'm Jasper."

"Annabelle." She took my hand, shook it firmly, and then gave me a curious look. "So what's your story, morning glory? This isn't really the type of concert anyone just attends on a whim."

I wasn't sure how to respond. I doubted she wanted to hear about how Greg had dragged me here against his own better judgment as a last-ditch effort to entertain his friend. The thought of Greg prompted me to turn and see if I could spot him or his friends. All I could see were black t-shirts and long hair, no recognizable faces among them. Annabelle turned around too, but gave me a confused look when she realized that she wasn't sure what she was looking for. Our eyes met again.

"Looking for someone?" she asked.

"Sorry," I muttered, trying to diffuse the awkward silence that was creeping in, "I guess I'm here because it's better than being back at home."

"Is home close?"

"Close? No," I answered. "A town in Western Pennsylvania that I'm sure you've never heard of. How about you?"

"Portland, born and raised." She was clearly proud of that statement. "You're a long way from Pennsylvania." I glanced down and noticed a little notepad with a pen clipped to it near my right hip. The notepad had a fancy leather-bound cover with the letter 'A' embossed in the center.

"Are you doing homework or something?" I asked.

Quickly, she reached across my lap and pushed the notepad under a windbreaker piled at the edge of the blanket.

"Homework, huh?" she asked, ignoring the question. "You must still be a college boy. Let me guess: senior at Penn State? Judging by your outfit, bloodshot eyes, and somewhat distorted social awareness, I'm going to guess a business major?"

She held her index finger out, moving it up and down as she studied me like a caveman specimen. And notwithstanding the college of choice (us Tundra folks had a disdain for Penn State), she was almost spot-on. I laughed at the cliché—did all business majors really look like this? Was being lumped together into one homogenous mass all that future Wall Street workers had to look forward to?

"Not bad," I replied. I imitated her index finger motion. "My turn. Given your condescending tone toward college students, your semi-rebellious haircut, and your 'I'm too cool to be with my peers so I'm going to sit on a blanket all by myself' attitude, I'm going to guess . . . former coke addict turned lesbian with an interest in astronomy?"

"Close enough, Jasper," she replied. "Doing my best to kick the habit while watching the stars. That's a very unique name by the way. Did you know that Jasper is also a type of mineral?"

"Mineralogy, huh?" I said. "Looks like I guessed the wrong scientific field. Also, everyone calls me Jass."

The mist from earlier was finally turning into a drizzle, and I could tell this was only the calm before the storm. After a few moments, my jeans were wet enough that I could feel their heaviness when I stretched my legs forward on Annabelle's blanket. Either Annabelle didn't notice the rain or she wasn't bothered by it, since, apart from pushing her notepad more completely underneath her windbreaker, she did nothing to cover herself. The rain didn't seem to affect any of the other people in the crowd, either. A few people were huddled underneath the main stage cover eating hot dogs, trying to stay dry, but everyone else seemed oblivious.

Over the next few minutes, Annabelle clued me in on some of the acts performing at the other stages. She knew everything. Soon she had exhausted her knowledge of the bands, and so I steered the conversation to more personal subjects. I imagined she must have more interesting things to say about herself than she did about the other artists here, and she seemed to welcome the change in topic.

I learned that she had graduated from Portland State with a journalism degree just the year before and was presently working a dead-end customer service job, since she hadn't managed to land anything more suited to her writing background.

"Newspapers are a dying industry," she said. "Most don't want to let any more passengers aboard their sinking ship." She brushed away any angst by telling me that she was grateful for her degree even if she hadn't located anything in the field yet. "Without that diploma staring me in the face, I'd probably have stopped writing the moment I left campus. But what about you? What's on deck after you graduate?"

"Most likely your standard nine to five. My dad's company has this one job that I will probably go after. I get the hint that it's sort of mine for the taking."

"What's the job?"

"I think it's somewhere in their corporate accounting division. Probably means I'll be sifting through earnings statements all day long. I'm not really sure."

"Oh my god!" Annabelle screamed. She cupped her face in her hands. "A job at your father's company that you don't even *understand*? That's so cliché! Please tell me you didn't actually accept the job yet." Even with the dramatic antics, she was still smiling, so her comments didn't bother me. It was actually refreshing for someone to challenge the inevitable path my life seemed bound to follow.

"Technically not yet," I said. I released my elbow and lay back fully on the blanket, staring at the sky, trying to find the correct words. "But what's the difference? You said yourself it's tough to find a steady job, so what's wrong with picking at the low-hanging fruit?"

"Nothing's wrong with that, as long as the fruit isn't poisonous. I make shit money at my job doing something a high-school grad can do. The only thing that keeps me sane is that I know it's temporary until I find something better. Trust me, if you settle into the comfortable suit-and-tie, corporate bullshit, you'll never leave. That shit pulls you under like quicksand. Please promise me you'll put up a fight."

Receiving advice from a peer was something I wasn't accustomed to, but I still promised, albeit with little motivation behind it. I took note of her declaration of her current state of life, though. I didn't pity her, and I'm sure if I responded with anything remotely resembling sympathy, she would make a snide comment back to me. Instead I looked at her full of curiosity, as both an individual and as a person not too far removed from my current situation as a near-graduate.

I continued to ask questions about anything: her life, her hobbies, her family. Asking in a sense meant I was avoiding revealing anything further about myself, but it didn't matter. I was rewarded with a myriad of honest responses that, cumulatively, described her unique philosophy toward life. She didn't give much in the way of details of any future writing, surprising given how much she seemed to enjoy the craft.

"Can I ask you a question?" I inquired at one point.

"Apparently," she responded, playfully swatting my side.

I noticed that we both lay on our sides now, no longer watching the stage but instead staring at each other. It was the first time she had touched me, something I had also thought about—but refrained from—doing. When she touched me, I did my best to play it cool, but in reality, the brief physical interaction sent a rush of adrenaline through my veins. My attraction to Annabelle had formed the moment she spoke to me, but this was the first time I began to undress her with my eyes. I glanced down to see a small amount of skin exposed between her shirt and her tight jeans. I thought about tapping her right there, just so I could touch her skin, but I decided it was too dangerous to double down on whatever she might have been insinuating. Better to just leave the door open to her making another move. Just to be sure.

"Even with the sucky journalism market, your miserable customer service job, and the Portland dating life, you still seem so damn positive about everything. Isn't there *anything* that bothers you?"

"Well sure," she responded, running her hands through her hair, as if digging far back into her memory bank, "but what's the point in dwelling? We're in our early twenties, Jass. If we're lucky we're going to have sixty or seventy more years to make tons of great memories. No sense on pining over the bad ones."

I was impressed. Most people are incapable of such insight, never mind sharing it with a stranger; I think people our age especially tended to be more worried about making a good first impression than speaking from the heart.

I continued watching Annabelle as she talked; she was constantly moving her legs around, almost as if she would leap up at any moment. Every time she shifted, I tried my best to inconspicuously peek down at her waist, which exposed more and more skin. At one point, she kicked so violently that her shirt rode right up her torso, and for a brief second I caught a glimpse of both her bra and underwear. They were matching dark blue, and I immediately looked away from her midriff, hoping to conceal the fact that I was getting hard. We had shifted close enough to each other that I could have leaned forward and kissed her right there. Plus, all she had to do was look down to see something poking through my jeans. But I was paralyzed with fear. I interpreted Annabelle's actions as flirting, especially when she slapped my leg, but a kiss was a bold move, one that I didn't have the guts to make quite yet.

Noticing my distraction, Annabelle ended the awkward pause by leaning forward and grabbing my shoulder. "Come on." She stood up.

"What about the—" I pointed, forgetting who was playing on stage "—the most underrated performer at the concert?"

"The problem with being underrated is that you tend to evoke really high expectations from your biggest fans. We'll probably end up disappointed."

She took off down the field, leaving her blanket, jacket and mysterious notepad behind. I gave the area one last look, wondering if we'd ever make our way back to that blanket again, or if Annabelle would return on her own to write a scathing note in that journal about the ugly drifter business major that she had finally managed to lose. Then I turned and raced after her, and eventually caught up.

"Here," she said and turned, grabbing my hand and pulling me in the direction of the lower stages. It wasn't a long-lasting embrace; within seconds the contact was broken. But for a brief instant I hesitated. Not because I didn't want to follow Annabelle, but because it was obvious that her hand grab had nothing to do with guiding me in the right direction. My heart raced, as I realized that the time would eventually come when I would need to make a move. Before this moment, everything was an experiment in flirtation, but now the signal was clear. The next move was mine.

It turned out that what I had seen of Konacks—a few stages and a concession stand—was only about half of what the concert had to offer. About a hundred yards from our stage, the trees behind the field ended, opening up to reveal two smaller stages and about fifty more people milling around or sitting on the wet ground. Only one stage was being used, by a solo guitarist who was playing so softly that at first I didn't even notice he was there. Annabelle did though, and she dragged me through the crowd to the front of the stage. I turned to see the rest of the audience paying little attention, which surprised me given how much he looked in his element.

"Can you see it?" she asked. I wasn't sure what 'it' was, so after I looked around for a minute or so, she pointed to the performer's hands. "Look at how his fingers are playing the guitar. They're perfectly still from the knuckles up. That's almost unheard of, given how many chords he's playing. And he's been playing for hours."

She was right. His fingers moved at a slow pace, but every chord was executed in the most natural way possible. He was singing, too, though even through the microphone the lyrics sounded more like a strong mumble than coherent sentences. Still, the immediate admiration I felt reminded me of the violinist from earlier.

"Who is this guy?" I asked, my eyes still glued to his hands. The music reminded me more of a softened bluegrass sound than the heavier music from the other bands. I tried deciphering the rhythm so that I could anticipate what notes would be coming next, but I couldn't find any consistency; it was as if the guy was making up notes and sounds on the spot. Yet they all sounded like they made sense within the context of the song, clearly demonstrating the type of talent that emerges after years of pouring your heart and soul into your music.

"His name is Blake Storling, but he goes by Sonic

Boom," she replied. "He's the founder of the festival."

"No way!" I turned and looked at the audience, which consisted of more people playing hacky sack and throwing Frisbees than watching. "But people are barely paying attention to him."

"You're right," she agreed, "because most people don't know who he is. Blake Storling is a visionary, a man who bet his entire financial well-being on the success of this concert. All because he loved music and imagined a place where local artists could gather and play for days, without all the headaches that come along with bigger venues. Sonic Boom is just an unknown folk artist with barely any fans."

"Why would he do that? Why the anonymity?"

"Look around you Jass." She turned around and extended her arms to the entire field. "Look what he created! If anyone here knew that this guy was responsible for all of this, they would probably flock to the stage out of some misguided sense of moral obligation, and then they'd miss out on the bands at the other stages. Storling doesn't care; he's happy singing about butterflies or whatever he's doing up there. He just wants to be a part of the experience, like everyone else."

She spoke like she had co-founded the concert herself, forming a defiant 'X' with her body, her legs spread out, her arms stretched to the sky. Her back was to me, and I inched toward her, close enough that I could smell the small patch of grass caked on her shirt from the lawn. Finally, I reached out, gently placing my hand on her lower back. Merely feeling the heat of her skin through her shirt aroused me again and I pulled my hand away.

"So what now?" I murmured. I was curious—not necessarily about what we were doing next, but whether or not Annabelle was an improviser or if there was a method to the madness. She looked around, and then up at the sky, but she never turned around. The drizzle was still a drizzle.

"I have something I want to show you." She grabbed

my hand again, and we took off. A part of me wanted to stay rooted and continue listening to Blake Storling, to hear the music of the man behind this entire experience. But it was a wonderful feeling to commit myself to the unknown.

Behind the stage stood a tiny wooden fence, with nothing on the other side but more grass. Annabelle hopped over and took off running, leaving me little time to hesitate. I jumped the fence and ran to catch up. After about twenty yards, the grass sloped downhill, and my running morphed into a fast skip.

Annabelle was still ahead of me, her long legs carrying her frame faster than mine. All I spotted ahead was a swampy marsh at the bottom of the hill, and as adventurous as Annabelle appeared, I couldn't imagine that was where she was heading. Suddenly, she planted one foot and pivoted ninety degrees into a group of trees. She stopped, waiting for me to catch up. When I reached her, I hunched over, gripping my knees.

"You could have warned me this was going to turn into a workout."

"Shh!" she hissed, slamming her finger to her lips. "We're not supposed to be here during the concert."

There was nothing around us but nature. Where exactly weren't we supposed to be?

She kept walking—tip-toeing, almost—and I followed. We spent the next few minutes creeping along in complete silence. I followed a few feet behind her, dodging thorn bushes and pushing branches away so they weren't hitting me in the face. Eventually the brush opened up, and nestled between all of the trees was a giant rock. Nothing else surrounded it, as if any branches or leaves that may have fallen in close proximity had been purposely brushed away. It took a couple seconds to register, but I finally realized that the rock was shaped like a heart. A broken one.

"What is this?"

For a while, Annabelle ignored me. She stared at the

rock, slowly circling it, examining every facet from every angle. About halfway around, she touched the rock, tracing her finger in various patterns along its surface. I edged forward to study it myself.

The rock was technically two structures—almost mirror images of one another—tan in color, with smooth limestone-like surfaces, separated at the top but nearly touching at the bottom. The sparse light that peeked through the trees served as a spotlight, accentuating the grooves and crevices marking the stone's surface.

"Its official name is Petunia. I had heard about this rock but I'd never actually seen it," she began. "The rock is supposedly a local legend because of its shape and location. Apparently over a dozen marriages are held at this spot every year."

"Why would anyone want to take their vows next to a damaged rock?"

"Because this rock is a symbol," she said. "It's embracing philosophy, nature, God, divine intervention, people, faith, love, sickness, everything! It's taking a chance on the fact that something is bigger than you, and making a commitment to someone that you're in this journey called life together, from beginning to end. So people come here, to this broken rock, to acknowledge that while they might not have the answers, they can at least accept that the person they love doesn't, either. Haven't you ever felt that way about something?"

I didn't answer and instead touched the rock. It was even smoother than it looked, and while it took the shape of a broken heart, it was a broken heart with no ridges or deformities. I continued to glide my hand over the rock until it reached the spot where Annabelle rested hers. She looked down, except this time, she didn't grab my hand. Instead, she gripped my shirt and pulled me closer. When she embraced me, pulling my lips to hers, she was aggressive, like she needed to do it. Immediately her mouth opened and our tongues entwined. I had forgotten all about the wonders of a new kiss, the anticipation of it all. It was like finishing a novel you had been dying to read for months. All I could think was, a*t last*.

Annabelle eventually fell back against the rock, opening her body to me, but at first I kept my hands at my sides. I wanted to explore all of her, her legs, her neck, her breasts, but I resisted. Instead I kept my eyes closed, focusing all of my energy on her crimson luscious lips. I could almost taste her black cherry chapstick from inches away. Annabelle's hands were gripping my shoulders, and when she finally began to move them down my back, every last ounce of willpower disappeared.

My hands mirrored hers, gliding along her sides until they were underneath her bottom, with only the denim of her jeans separating our skin. I hoisted her on top of my hips, her thick swath of hair—though short—still swinging forward and hitting me in the face. She whisked it back and leaned forward again, her chest pressed against mine, her legs locked around my waist. She kissed harder, and I grabbed harder. After touching nearly every other inch of her body, my hands slid underneath her shirt, finally reaching her breasts. I slowed down a bit, slightly rolling my hands across them until they reached behind again, when I gripped the soft smooth skin of her back. At that moment, I wanted nothing but to take her clothes off, see what she looked like in nothing but her blue underwear. But instead, a moment later, Annabelle let go of me, unwinding her legs and breathing hard against my chest. Two seconds later, she pulled away entirely.

"We should get back to the concert."

I didn't care about the concert. I wanted to make love, right there on the rock, to relive that same sense of bewilderment that I experienced the night I lost my virginity nearly four years ago. My toes curled as I pictured each second of the act: how we'd likely move from the rock to the ground, ignoring the sticks and pebbles grinding into our skin as we came together.

As if on cue, the music from hundreds of yards away started to elevate, as did the clapping and cheering that followed. Annabelle motioned toward the edge of the woods, and I sighed and nodded. Taking a deep breath, I grabbed *her* hand, and we took the same path back, eventually reaching the top of the hill and climbing back over the small wooden fence. A few of the performers were still there, but, as I knew he would be, Blake Storling was gone. The crowds had moved to surround the other stages, and there was no one near the concession stand anymore.

"You won't want to miss this," she said, and led me back to the main stage. "The finale is the best part."

I didn't know what we were about to see, but something told me that leaving my fate in Annabelle's hands was the best thing I could do. So I followed her across the field.

And then the skies opened.

****

Dear readers:

To the 8,000 of you who frequent this blog (Is it that many? Really?)—whether you know me on a personal level, professional level, or just don't know me at all—you are aware that I like to keep my personal life and my blogging life separate. Yes, blogging is a deep-rooted hobby of mine, but I've tried my best to avoid any talk of past lovers, first-dates or one-night stands. For me, I always thought it was more interesting to discuss the musicians, writers, filmmakers, and painters that come and go in this city. There are enough writers out there who can entertain/bore you with their roller coaster love lives. So forgive me for taking a detour today to discuss something that happened to me, your humble Miss Mezzanine.

This past weekend, I attended the 2002 Konacks Music and Arts Festival here in Portland. Much like last year, the music offered an eclectic combination of local bands, some faring better than others. Surprisingly, the ones that headlined the show were the least memorable, almost 'phoning in' their performances, which allowed a few of the smaller artists to shine. I attended the concert solo this time; last year, I had embarked with a random group of individuals, one of whom had little control over his alcoholic intake, forcing us to leave the concert two hours earlier than I would have liked. So this year I politely told any friends that they should attend without me and we'd meet up later. I took only a blanket and my notepad, and expected a relaxing time. What I didn't expect was an interaction with a modern-day Romeo Montague.

The concert was nearing its end, and Donegal was the only musician left I didn't want to miss. I arrived at his stage just as it began to rain; my heavy burgundy blanket was getting soaked, even from the light drizzle. I watched in awe, wondering how this performer hadn't broken out of his local roots yet, when a young guy was suddenly towering over me, right in front of the spot I had claimed for myself on the lawn. His name was Jasper, though he later informed me that friends call him "Jass" (or Jas? Jazz? – I guess I never got the official spelling). He appeared harmless, so I invited him to join me.

Our conversation began with some stereotypical small-talk, the sort of banter that disappears from your memory minutes after parting. But Jasper didn't seem to be interested in asking a lineup of questions just to make the time go faster; he wanted to learn about me. When I told him I went to Portland State, he wanted to know *why* I went there. When I reminisced about my first concert, he asked me to describe my entire experience (which I imagine was less inspired by his curiosity than it was about giving me a chance to relive one of my favorite childhood moments). Our conversation eventually took a more personal turn, but his methods never changed. I found myself telling him things that I hesitate to tell even my closest friends. He exhibited such a trustworthy persona that the most intimate details of my life came pouring off of my tongue with little restraint.

Jasper was keen on asking me questions but at first only reciprocated when I pushed him. He was your stereotypical college senior, realizing that the era of misguided youth was coming to an end. I offered what little advice I could as someone who has only lived one post-college year thus far. He listened intently, though, giving me more credence than I likely deserved, and for a minute I saw a glimpse of myself in him: a free spirit unsure of how to adjust to a life not suited for his talents.

In spite of his initial resistance, he slowly opened up, revealing himself to be a thoughtful and selfless soul, well beyond his years. We continued to talk while Donegal— who no longer held my attention—continued to play, until suddenly a shock of spontaneity burst through my veins. Talking was pleasant, to be sure, but there was an unspoken sexual tension building between the two of us, and sitting there on a blanket in front of a hundred strangers was no way to explore it. So I grabbed his hand and led him to a place of solitude, so that whatever we were feeling could be defined, however wonderful or scary it might turn out. For twenty minutes, we did just that: explored. I won't go into all of the details (those are between Jass and me), but it ended in a kiss that shocked my nerves from head to toe, one so passionate that it wiped out every mediocre and meaningless kiss that has come before it.

When the concert ended, neither of us were ready to leave, but the universe seemed to be pushing us in entirely opposite directions. I suppose we could have taken our urges to the next level: had sex all night at my apartment and then finished it off with an awkward breakfast and wave goodbye. But I couldn't let that happen—our night deserved better. Something sparked between Jass and me, and turning it into a one-night romp would have cheapened the whole experience. So what did I do? I gave him one last kiss and said goodbye, with rain pouring down my cheeks and his smile still glistening in the moonlight. I wanted my encounter with him to end in the same mysterious way that it began.

As we parted, several questions ran through my mind. What's next? Will we go out again? Stay in touch? Try a long-distance relationship? What's funny is, all I had to do was mutter the words "Miss Mezzanine" and he'd be able to find me in two minutes, regardless of where in the country he was actually from. There are zero other results if you do an internet search of my blog title (testify!), so it's not a matter of if or how he could find me. But again, for some reason, I resisted. The fact is, Jasper lives at the other end of the country. And knowing that the odds of recreating what we shared are slim to none, I didn't try to force a reconnection.

So instead, I leave my encounter with Jass as a bottled memory of bliss, a two-hour joyride of infatuation, one that I'll likely never experience again. And that's ok. He sparked a level of excitement in me that I never thought I could unleash. And if my time with Jass ends with this post, then I promise you, my faithful readers, that it was a journey worth taking.

Keep a lookout for my full concert review in the next few days.

With love,

Miss Mezzanine

2

Greg and I just finished going through airport security, making our way down the Portland airport terminal in silence. I stood still on the moving walkway with my tiny carry-on, attempting to soak in my last few moments in the city. Greg on the other hand—with his backpack hoisted over his shoulders—hurried alongside of it on the regular floor, rushing to a gate that was probably filled to the brim with waiting passengers. I looked out the giant window and saw nothing but empty land leading to Mt. Hood, a beautiful glacier-covered anomaly that stretched higher than any mountain I'd ever seen. I smiled, thinking how appropriate it was that the last Portland landmark I would see had served as the backdrop for the Konacks Festival the night before.

"Enjoy the view while you can buddy," Greg said. The moving walkway ended and we both now stood together, directly in front of our gate, which was just as crowded as I expected. "In just a few hours, the real world awaits us."

The thought of scribbling homework assignments in my three-ring binder prompted the same nausea I felt at the concession stand last night, so I chose to ignore Greg's reference. The flight had already started to board; I dug in my pocket and reached for my boarding pass again. As I did, I noticed a man still seated in the waiting area, typing frantically on his laptop. He wore suit pants and a jacket, clenching a cup of coffee between his thighs, laptop on his knees. It made me uncomfortable; I wanted to just hold the guy's coffee cup so he could finish what he was doing.

"Look at this guy," I whispered to Greg. "Think that'll be you, soon?"

Greg glanced at the guy and smiled. "I hope so," he said. "Business attire in an airport terminal? Probably on his way back from a business meeting with a top-tier client. My guess is he pulls in a hundred grand a year, easy."

"Yeah, but all the traveling? You want to be one of those people living out of your suitcase eleven months out of the year?"

"Hmm," he thought, tapping his fingers on his closed lips, "traveling the country on your company's dime, making six figures, and never having to pay for your own meals? Sign me up." He paused. "After all, not all of us have a comfy seat waiting for us at daddy's firm."

I punched his shoulder, knowing his comment was meant in jest. Greg and I both studied business, but he was much more determined than I was to enter the world of finance: the colorful trading room floors, flashing stock-ticker screens, stress-filled all-nighters. Working in Pittsburgh long-term enticed him, and so we made a few trips downtown together last semester so he could check out some potential firms. At one point I offered to introduce him to my father, but he refused, almost out of spite, stating his hatred for favors of any kind. Instead he applied to a few other companies and ultimately landed an internship, which he began this past January.

My distraction ended when I noticed the last group of preferred passengers boarding the plane. Then the gate agent called our group. Greg and I stood at the very end of the line, taking advantage of those final few moments to stretch our legs. Luckily our seats were in the very back row, so we could enjoy conversing or napping without people kicking the back of our heads during the flight. We took our seats, and my belt was not even fastened before Greg opened his mouth.

"So that girl you were with was pretty cute, huh?" He asked the question casually, although I imagined it had been on his mind all day.

"Huh?" I replied, pretending as if I hadn't heard him. I needed time to recover from the series of images flashing through my brain: Annabelle playfully kicking her legs on the red blanket; Annabelle standing, arms-extended, in front of Sonic Boom's stage; Annabelle lying against the rock. Greg knew I had heard his question, since he didn't bother asking twice. I tried looking away from his penetrating gaze.

"What," Greg said, lightly pushing me, "you think I didn't notice her?"

"Eh, she was average," I lied, pursing my lips and shrugging him off. Nothing about Annabelle was standard, but the thought of telling that to someone else, even my best friend, wasn't an option. "She was cute in that artsy sort of way, but nothing special." With every word that came out of my mouth, I started to panic. What exactly had Greg seen, and how much did he know? I should have figured he might spot us on the blanket, but nothing had happened up to that point, apart from innocent flirting. Could he have seen us hop the fence and sprint down the hill toward the swamp? Did he know about the rock? Did he see us kissing again when the concert was over? But I couldn't ask anything, since that would merely lead to incriminating myself further.

Greg only nodded, leaning back against the headrest and shutting his eyes. Relieved, I reached into my book bag and pulled out the Thomas Jefferson biography I had borrowed from the library for the trip. I doubted I'd be able to read much on the flight—I had a tendency to get airsick—but I decided to give it a try. Restlessness crept in after only a few pages though. We still hadn't taken off yet.

"I don't want to come back here, Jass." Greg spoke with his eyes still closed. "If I come home, it'll be too easy to settle, and then I don't think I'll ever leave again."

I set my book down on my lap. "Then don't come home. No one's forcing you."

Greg inhaled deeply. For a moment it looked like he was going to begin a rant, but he only exhaled, dragging out the breath as long as he could. He pursed his lips. "Remind me of this conversation even if my internship doesn't springboard into anything."

"I will." It was all I could say. And just like that, the conversation ended. I attempted to read again, but now was nowhere close to the reading mood. I pressed the call button directly above my head to summon the flight attendant. When she arrived, I put my acting face on, looking as nervous and awkward as I possibly could.

"Miss, can I please have something to drink?"

"Sure, let me get you a glass of water."

I stopped her before she could leave. "I was hoping for something a bit stiffer. Shot of whiskey, maybe?"

"Sir there's no alcohol served prior to takeoff," she replied. "We'll start beverage service once we reach our cruising altitude." She glanced at my apparel from head to toe; it wasn't difficult to pin me as a scruffy college student. "And the whiskey is ten dollars, cash only."

I thanked her anyway and laughed to myself as she walked away. How ironic, to spend several hundred on a spring break trip and then not even have enough money to buy myself a shot to ease the trip back. This was going to be a long flight.

The plane touched down in Pittsburgh thirty minutes

late, so my post-nap grumpiness was compounded by the fact that I wouldn't be getting back to campus until after nearly two o'clock in the morning. Normally I wouldn't care, but the thought of attending my first class after break on five hours of sleep was unsettling.

Thankfully our flight's luggage was already circling the baggage claim when we arrived. I noticed my suitcase approach us on the conveyor belt, and though it was clearly marked, Greg let it pass by and didn't help me retrieve it. He had barely said two words to me since the flight, and I could almost feel his cold demeanor oozing in my direction. At first I attributed it to jet-lagged crankiness, but gradually, more troubling thoughts crept into my head. He hadn't mentioned Annabelle beyond those initial questions on the flight, and I hoped he didn't ask any more. But was he angry at me? I was too afraid to ask. Fortunately, if there was one saving grace, it was that Greg had driven to the airport, and so I knew our awkward silence could be plugged up with some late-night radio.

The walk from the terminal to the car passed by quickly. Greg had managed to grab one of the first spots near the exit when we parked five days ago. We hopped in his Camry and began inching our way through the stop-and-go airport traffic until we finally made our way to the last gate. The moment we hit the freeway, he gunned it, and we were suddenly flying toward campus at eighty miles per hour.

"So are you going to tell Carrie?"

It was the first time since last Saturday that I had heard my girlfriend's name spoken aloud. The sound of it felt like a dagger in my stomach.

"Tell Carrie what?"

"Come on," he said, shaking his head, "you know what. That you were flirting with that girl at the concert."

I didn't respond, because although Greg obviously knew more than I had hoped, he clearly didn't know the whole story, and I didn't want to risk incriminating myself further.

I trusted my best friend more than anyone, but he was also very close with Carrie. After all, it was Greg who was partly responsible for the two of us meeting at a campus charity event last year. I recalled the exact moment I met her at the event: standing around one of those toxic-pink-colored punchbowls, pretending I was heavily involved in whatever cause they were supporting that day. In actuality, Greg had dragged me there to serve as a wingman, to help him talk to a girl he was pursuing. I had obliged, but his plan never came to fruition. Greg had just run off to the bathroom when a girl in dress pants and a button-down shirt approached me.

"I couldn't help but notice you've been hanging around this punchbowl for the last twenty minutes," the girl said. "You realize everyone here thinks you're a chaperone?"

"Oh god, really?" I asked, "Well fine then. I'm just keeping you guys in check. These charity events can get out of hand pretty quickly."

She smiled, and poured herself a cup of punch. I grabbed it from her hand and took a sip.

"Yumm."

She laughed and took it right back from me. Neither one of us left the punchbowl for the rest of the night. I totally lost track of Greg, which I guess makes me a bad friend, since I also never asked him about the girl he had been pursuing. Instead, I left the party bragging that this really smart, really funny girl I had never met before had given me her cell phone number.

Carrie was attractive to begin with, but she was also the kind of attractive that increased over time. Within a few weeks of dating, I remembered asking myself how I had managed to avoid meeting her, given that her looks would have stood out among the other co-eds in my class. Over time though I discovered that her intelligence—which seemed to grow leaps and bounds with every conversation—personified that beauty, adding a layer to

Carrie that most girls at Tundra didn't possess.

"There's nothing to tell," I finally replied. "We had an interesting conversation and nothing more. No need to get Carrie involved."

Lying wasn't necessarily difficult—we all told the occasional fib to avoid confrontation—but lying about the concert, and Annabelle in particular, felt like a betrayal. There were two types of lies: lies about things that didn't happen and lies about things that did. The first is the artist's lie: the lie that requires the right, creative side of the brain to fabricate a story, whether to avoid trouble or to explain an awkward set of circumstances. The second was more about *hiding* than lying, and those ones were much worse. Making up something was ok in small doses, since, after all, it never happened. But suppressing the truth was always a recipe for disaster. After only one or two sentences with Greg, my stomach began to churn. I knew that these wouldn't be the first lies I was going to tell. But I did my best to try and convince myself that they were necessary lies.

I turned away and planted my face against the window, hoping to dissolve the conversation. Knowing I had to face Carrie soon was one thing; having Greg suspiciously breathing down my neck was something else entirely. It was something I hadn't prepared for, and something that could, therefore, go horribly wrong.

Fortunately, my tactic worked. Greg didn't mention Carrie or 'the girl' for the rest of ride. At some point I dozed off again, and when I awoke, we were just pulling into campus. It was pitch dark, but I could still make out the giant T-shaped red lamppost at the school gate, welcoming us back.

Greg and I shared an apartment within the only non-dorm complex on campus. It was a hollow square building, with architecture that reminded me of the other classical Romanesque buildings on the campus. Our apartment was on the second floor, so we had access to a balcony that stretched around the entire complex. We were lucky; there was a lottery to get into one of the sixteen apartments in the building, and my name was the first one drawn. It was the only time in my life I can recall winning a game of chance.

We parked right in front of our building, and I extended my arms in a long stretch. Greg, on the other hand, didn't wait for me and hurried inside before I had even gotten out of the car. He left the front door ajar, and I shuffled in after him, throwing my suitcase on the ground right inside the door. I heard another door slam further inside the apartment. Greg hadn't even bothered to say goodnight.

The living room was just as we had left it, which in fairness was cleaner than most dwellings within a fifty mile radius. The two of us were overly tidy compared to our peers; there was rarely a potato chip crumb or empty beer can to be found, and any arguments between us were usually a result of one of us cleaning the *wrong* way, as opposed to not cleaning at all. The remote controls rested on the coffee table just where I had left them, and though I was tempted to pop in a DVD, my body was begging for sleep.

As I approached my bedroom, I noticed that the door was slightly ajar. I pushed it open to find a figure lying on my bed.

"Carrie."

She was lying there, smiling, her eyes half-closed.

"Hi," she muttered, exhaling a yawn. She stretched her arms. "You're back late." She pushed the covers off of her body, exposing a pair of blue pajamas, which I had bought for her birthday last year. The knots that had formed in my stomach during the car ride with Greg began to resurface.

"What's wrong?" she asked. I realized that I was fortunate that Carrie was half-asleep; had she been a bit more awake, she could have read my guilt from five feet away.

I shook my head. "Everything's fine," I lied, "just exhausted." I couldn't think of anything else to say; my mind was spinning, attempting to craft answers to questions that Carrie hadn't even asked me yet. I pictured Annabelle lying on that bed, instead of Carrie, and how enthusiasm, rather than fear and uncertainty, would rush through my veins at the sight of her. I *knew* everything about last night was wrong on some level, but suddenly I was having difficulty brushing away my feelings and focusing instead on what was supposed to be a thrill at seeing Carrie.

"Well come to bed," she said. "My parents drove me back a couple hours early tonight, so I thought I'd surprise you." Her eyes shut again, and she kicked her body to the side, making room for me. As soon as I got into bed, she turned and faced the wall; after ten months of sleeping together in the same bed, I knew that meant the lights were out for good.

I felt paroled for the time being, able to fall asleep without having to dance around my experience at the concert, since Carrie was likely to ask about it sooner or later. Normally I'd roll over and wrap my arms around her, but I couldn't tonight. Instead I lay on my back and stared at the ceiling, listening to Carrie's rhythmic breaths. I had thought I'd be glad to be home, but suddenly I wished I was back on the plane, so I could order something, *anything*, to help erase Annabelle from my memory.

I awoke to an empty bed and a note next to my pillow from Carrie, saying we'd meet up later in the afternoon, after our classes. I had to drag myself out of bed; my fidgeting around throughout the night had amounted to fewer than three hours of sleep. The thought of skipping my first class was tempting, but disrupting my routine would spark even more questions, so I darted out the door with about twenty minutes to spare. Immediately upon stepping out into the daylight, I smiled. For the first time in a week, the Tundra landscape grabbed my attention, a nice reminder that all vacations circle back home.

Tundra University was located just north of Pittsburgh, right on the border where Western Pennsylvania's hard-edged liberal city met that conservative-filled, Bible-belt area. Most of Tundra's students lived within an hour or two of the school. Carrie and I both fell in that camp, each growing up in Pittsburgh suburbs. Tundra was one of those campuses that city kids loved: far enough away to claim independence, but close enough to zip home every so often for a home-cooked meal. In fact, to my knowledge, Greg was the only student from anywhere west of the Great Plains. When we first met, I asked him why he chose Tundra out of all the colleges in the country, and he responded with, "They had the nicest brochure."

Suddenly my cell phone rang. I flipped it open to read 'DAD', but hesitated hitting 'send'. Doing so likely meant a crash course in some social or political subject, matters that neither impacted nor interested me. Still, I knew I could always cut the call short when I got to my class, which might not be the case if he called back later. I hit 'send.'

"Hi dad."

"I spoke with Frank Harrison yesterday evening," my father began, in such a casual tone that it was as if we were somehow continuing a conversation that hadn't ended. "He's conference-hopping this entire week but should be grounded by Monday."

"That's great, dad."

"You're goddamn right it's great. I told him that you were going to be caught up with final exams and whatnot during the last week of April, so he said he can interview you next Friday for a spot in his group. Do you think you could switch around any conflicting classes so that you can make it in for a few hours?"

"Sure. I should be able to talk to my—"

"Because Frank's a really busy guy, Jasper. And he's

going out on a limb for me—for *you*—by putting your name at the front of the line. You'd better rearrange your schedule. Everything else is a distraction at this point, anyway."

Great, the 'everything else is a distraction' lecture. As a kid, behavioral training (my dad's term for 'learning your manners') took precedence; everything else was a distraction. As a junior high student, running track or playing baseball shaped my future; everything else was a distraction. In high school, it was college. Now in college, it's a job.

"It's on my calendar, dad. Writing it down now." I gestured a fake scribble in midair as I continued to trot along the pathway toward my first class. Mentally, I scrambled for a new topic of conversation, because unless I switched the subject soon, I knew he'd spend the next fifteen minutes describing the current market outlook and the statistical ramifications of not landing a job immediately upon graduation.

"How's mom?" I asked, trying my best to change the subject. Not that it mattered too much; I knew the two barely spoke, their marriage a facade of sustainability more than a committed relationship.

"She's fine, busy doing projects around the house. I'm sure she's awake now; you should give call her when we get off the phone."

"I will," I lied as I began climbing the steps to McLaren Hall, where my first class was held. I waved to a couple students I recognized from my class. "My eight o'clock starts in about two minutes though, so I have to run. I'll talk to you later."

"Don't forget about next Friday. I mean it." His authoritative voice returned, any empathy regarding my mother long gone. I only nodded, not actually answering, and pressed the 'end' button down hard on my phone. By now, all of the other students were piling into the room, and I jogged to catch up, the echoing sounds of my footsteps reminding me that spring break was now, officially, over. *Just three weeks*, I thought, counting down the days until I graduated. *But then what? What do I even have to look forward to?*

My first class that morning—Advertising & Ethics—defined monotony. My professor, an aging former corporate attorney, over-emphasized the 'Ethics' part and swept 'Advertising' under the rug. This resulted in a course more suitable for highly-focused law school hopefuls than business major undergrads. I was frequently forced to hide my disinterest, since for some reason the professor took a liking to me, often calling on me to answer his random fill-in-the-blank questions. I prayed that he'd back off today, since neither my brain nor eyes exhibited a learning pulse. Thankfully, he let me be.

As soon as the class ended, I rushed out of the room and toward the campus cafeteria. Having an apartment with a kitchen meant I didn't usually frequent the place, but I knew Carrie would be there. We weren't supposed to talk again until the afternoon, but I thought preemptively visiting her would somehow make me look better, even though Carrie hadn't suspected anything was wrong.

Weaving my way around dozens of freshmen—who, I might add, looked a lot calmer and more collected than I had at that age—I reached the cafeteria entrance, where the smell of hydrogenated oils and grease-filled steam overwhelmed me. Even entering the hallway was enough; I knew that I'd need to shower as soon as I got back to my apartment in order to rid myself of the smell. I spotted Carrie at one of the rectangular tables near the front of the cafeteria. She sat by herself at a table draped with a colorful banner announcing "Spring Cotillion" She was scribbling notes on a piece of paper and at first didn't even notice me hovering over her.

"Don't you ever get a break?" I joked, pulling up a chair

next to her. She looked up and smiled.

"Yeah well, if I don't sell these tickets, no one else will."
She sighed and immediately went back to writing her notes.

Carrie was the Vice President of the Campus Outreach
Committee, a small group of highly-focused students
responsible for all the major events happening throughout
campus: anything from movie nights to trivia contests to
scavenger hunts. Carrie had signed up for the Committee
freshman year and ascended its ranks so quickly that much
of her extra-curricular time was spent planning things.

"How long have you been here?" I asked.

"Since eight-thirty."

"Why don't you leave the tickets and we'll go for a
walk?"

She rolled her eyes and sighed, a combined gesture I
encountered every now and then over the past couple
months. By now, Carrie's reactions implied more than her
words. Before she even spoke, I knew Carrie didn't want to
budge. I pressed on anyway.

"Three weeks left until we graduate, Carrie," I said "and
when we do, no one's going to remember the Spring
Cotillion or Beach Party Bingo or any of this. Don't kill
yourself worrying about it."

"Easy to say, coming from the man who never once
participated in any fun extracurricular activity his whole
college career."

"That's not true!" I jokingly pleaded. "Remember the
Ultimate Frisbee gig?"

"Do two games, one of which was called on account of
weather, count as a gig?"

I attempted to tickle her sides, but she pushed me away.

"Jass, please," she said, "you're catching me at the worst
possible time. I have thirty minutes before the cafeteria
closes to set up for lunch, and I need to empty out at least
twenty more tickets. And then I have prep work for my one
thirty that I didn't even start yet."

I backed off. Carrie's dedication to all things academic wasn't anything new; I just didn't realize how quickly she would fall back into her routine after spring break. And if her stress proved anything, it was that my trip had escaped her memory by now, which meant that she was unlikely to corner me on any specifics of the concert. Thank God for small favors.

I kissed her on the cheek and stroked her arm for a few seconds before letting go. I then left the building, feeling the sudden warmth of the sun shining down on me. During the few minutes that I was in the cafeteria, the clouds had shifted. It was the first sign that the spring was finally approaching, and that the cold, gross weather we'd been experiencing for the past three months was nearing an end. It also meant that I could walk across campus as much as I wanted, without worrying about getting drenched or frozen. And that's just what I did, my next class be damned.

A few nights later, my friend Jake from the other end of our apartment complex decided to throw a 'grown up people party,' allegedly in preparation for our entry into adulthood. This wasn't meant to be the typical kegger; everyone had to dress up in business casual clothing or better. All traces of a normal college party (plastic cups, beer pong, loud music) would be replaced with contemporary, middle-aged paraphernalia (wine glasses, backgammon, Mozart played on repeat). Carrie was thrilled to attend, relishing the idea of prancing around like a young professional. I was more apathetic, not outright embracing the party's theme (though I did wear a nice pair of khakis) but at least looking forward to a change in the usual frenetic pace of college parties.

Carrie brought her outfit over and dressed up at my place; she sported a navy blue cocktail dress she had worn to her cousin's wedding a couple months before. I glanced admiringly at her legs, displayed in all their long, lean athleticism below her dress. She wasn't one to often show skin, usually sporting sweatpants or jeans to her classes. That reserved attitude was probably my favorite part about her. She knew she could show herself off at any time but chose not to regularly showcase her best features, instead reserving them for special occasions.

"You look stunning," I told her. "Expect some gazing and gawking tonight."

"And you're not jealous?"

"Nope, not a bit. It earns me a sort of a universal bragging right, actually."

Carrie lightly punched my shoulder.

Over the last four days, Carrie had loosened up a bit—likely due to the fact that she met her dance ticket quota by the end of our first day back. She even apologized for being so stressed out in the cafeteria, which then of course made me feel guilty all over again, since I was the one who should be apologizing. Instead, I helped to facilitate our return to the Tundra lifestyle—Thursday spaghetti nights, Friday movie nights in her dorm. In the interim, I tried to block out any memories of Annabelle. Unfortunately, even after nearly a whole week, that wasn't getting any easier.

As soon as Carrie and I were ready to leave, I knocked on Greg's door to wake him up from his nap. He looked like he could barely walk, let alone socialize at a party full of people, but in typical Greg fashion, he readied himself up in just a few minutes, sporting a polished suit complete with a fancy red tie and clean-shaven face. I grabbed the bottle of Pinot Noir that I had bought earlier—my knowledge of wine was limited to 'red' vs. 'white', but according to the liquor store cashier, this Noir was the best option in my ten-to-fifteen dollar price range—and the three of us set off for Jake's apartment.

"Gentlemen, and lady!" Jake greeted us at the door. His legs were crossed as he leaned casually against the wall, and he sported a top hat that nearly hit the ceiling. "Please, come on in. I would just ask you kindly leave your shoes in the foyer. If you head past the East Wing, we have a variety of white and red wines at the bar and an assorted cheese platter on the veranda."

The three of us laughed at Jake's aristocratic imitation, but he actually looked in his element, all dressed up and proper.

"You know," he said, "I've been saying that to everyone, and I think I've finally nailed my delivery." Jake guided us past the foyer (though it was actually a small entranceway with a bunch of sports jerseys piled on the floor) and into the dining room. No sign of a veranda, but an actual cheese platter and about a dozen or so bottles of different wines covered the table, which was still the same folded up polyethylene table we had used to play Beer Pong as freshmen. This was as close to a *Great Gatsby* moment as we were likely to get while unemployed and living in college housing.

I picked up a corkscrew from the table and struggled to pop open my bottle. Carrie laughed at me, ripping the corkscrew out of my hand and finishing the job. She poured me a glass, and then one for herself. Greg was preoccupied, so she took the liberty of pouring him one, too, nudging him to take it when she had finished.

"Cheers," Carrie said, clinking the tops of our glasses.

"What are we toasting to?" Greg asked, swishing the wine around.

"How about the fact that it's the first time either of you uncultured losers are actually drinking a glass of wine?" Carrie joked.

"Hardy har-har," Greg replied, hitting Carrie on her side. "How about we just celebrate that it's one of the last times that we'll all be doing this together."

My eyes locked on his. What was he implying? He didn't notice, instead clinking my glass, followed by Carrie's. I took my first sip. Tasty. Much sweeter than the other wines

I'd tried before, which were few. I swallowed, and the heaviness of the thick, non-carbonated alcohol burned down my esophagus.

"Why anyone chooses this shit over a brewsky is just beyond me," Greg remarked, making a face. I turned to Carrie to see what her reaction would be, but her attention had shifted to a group of girls across the room.

"I'll be right back," she said. "I'm going to say hi to a few of the girls." She walked away. When she was out of sight, I turned to Greg.

"What did you mean when you said that this is the last time we'd all be together?" I asked.

"Whoa there killer," Greg responded. "No need to get all serious. Look around you. Look at this scene. I seriously doubt the three of us will be basking in this type of environment once we graduate. We'll be slaving away at our jobs and won't have time for any fun like this."

"And what makes you so sure about that, huh?" I asked, taking another drink, this one bigger than the last. "Maybe our jobs, whatever they are, will be painless and low key. Not everybody's career makes them miserable, you know."

Greg laughed. "Well I guess you're right, but don't expect that job at daddy's firm to be easy street. Those boys there are like ruthless sharks."

At the word 'daddy,' my first instinct was to splash Greg's face with the remaining wine in my glass; however, I was in no position to dispute the validity of his comments. His general arrogance aside, my father's work ethic was unmatched, and he expected the same from his employees. In some cases, he'd spend twelve-hour days at the office, returning home just as grumpy as he had left in the morning, complaining about how twenty percent of the employees (including himself, obviously) did eighty percent of the work.

"That attitude probably just applies to certain divisions," I responded, although in actuality I knew little about my father's firm, apart from third-hand information I gleaned from conversations with him. "I seriously doubt they'd expect their new hires to work like dogs right away."

"Jesus Christ!" Greg exclaimed, but still with a smile. "You're depressing me! This is a party! We're here to have fun! Take a drink—no, take two drinks—to the fact that you have a job in the wings that most of us would kill for, and you don't even have to do anything to claim it other than show up for the fucking interview!"

Greg's resentment—or perhaps it was jealousy— annoyed me, so I chose not to respond and instead deferred to taking another drink. The classical music began to pick up, and I noticed Carrie's roommate Stacey standing nearby talking to another girl and laughing extremely loudly. Stacey was much taller than Carrie, closer to Greg's height really. Her height combined with her tendency to talk at a decibel level that could wake the dead created an overbearingness that tested the patience of even the most Zen of students. And I decidedly did not practice Zen.

Greg looked annoyed, as though their mere presence was preventing him from unleashing a fury of life advice on me. Or maybe it was because (like me) he could barely tolerate Stacey, her faux feminism and general disdain for the male sex always trumping any attempt at being polite. Still, rather than talk over the pair, Greg chose to engage.

"Stacey," Greg said, "isn't there some political event you should be protesting at or something? Some kind of women's rights meeting?"

"Screw you Greg," Stacey glared, her eyes filled with anger. I would often call Stacey 'the gauntlet', because gaining access to Carrie—even in the privacy of her own bedroom—often meant an intense interrogation by Stacey, first, filled with deadly barbs intended to push me over the edge. She always came equipped with dozens of condescending follow-up questions to my basic statements, like 'Well didn't you just go there?', or 'How am I supposed to know where Carrie is, I'm not her babysitter.' I truly believed that Stacey's entire existence rested upon proving to as many people as she could that she was unlikeable.

"Where's your partner in crime?" Greg asked, referring to Carrie. Stacey shrugged, just as the girl she had been talking to drifted away.

"Well," Greg continued, "maybe you can offer some insight. Jass here is suffering from some sort of philosophical life crisis. Must have been paying too much attention to those John Stuart Mill books in his Intro to Philosophy class."

"Who is John Stuart Mill?" she asked.

"You see," he continued, ignoring her question, "Jass and I are having an intense argument about what life is going to be like after we graduate. I think that it's pretty easy to slide into a comfortable, low-stress job, find a nice person to settle with, white picket fences, the whole nine yards. Jass keeps telling me that I'm crazy, that it's all going to be incredibly difficult, and that I'm taking my situation for granted. Will you please set my misguided friend here straight?"

Ugh, I hated Greg when he did shit like this. It was an old tactic of his; taking the reverse position in a debate. He always argued that when two people had a disagreement and sought verification from a third party, the person who initially stated their views was picked as 'right' less than half the time. But I played along and didn't refute that the roles were completely opposite.

"Wait," she responded, pointing to me, "you're like, super smart. At least that's what Carrie tells me. I bet you're probably going to be a famous Bill Gates-type or something. Start an environmentally-friendly, renewable energy business or something like that."

"Well he's definitely smart and talented," Greg interrupted. "There's no doubt about that."

"Why do you think it'll be so easy?" Stacey asked Greg. I

could tell by the tone of her voice that this wasn't out of curiosity, but as a setup to another condescending question.

"Don't answer that Greg," I interjected. "You're walking into a pile of quicksand if you do."

Stacey rolled her eyes. "No need to be a jerk Jass," she said. "Although I doubt whether either of you has much in the way of cohesive arguments, I'll agree with Jass on this one for the first time in my life. You're rowing up shit's creek without a paddle if you think it gets easier after this."

"Well, I'm a huge fan of democracy, and it looks like the majority has spoken." Greg turned to me, clinking our glasses again. "Here's to you, Jass, for once again proving me wrong." I forced a smile. Eventually, Stacey wandered away, and I took the opportunity to tear into him.

"Trying to prove a point or something, Greg?" My glass of wine was empty, but within seconds of noticing, Greg had grabbed the bottle and was refilling both of our glasses.

"Just that you're floating in a cloud of denial if you don't realize how good you have it compared to the rest of us," he responded. "And I could ask you where all of this fantasy bullshit is coming from, but I can already guess. It's from your precious Portland girl, isn't it?"

"No," I replied, lowering my voice, "and I didn't think we were going to talk about her anymore."

"Yeah, I know, and I wasn't going to bring her up. But I was also hoping you would come clean, at least with me."

"Come clean about what, Greg?"

"Don't fucking insult me Jass. We went to the concert *together*, remember? I kept an eye out for you, like a responsible friend. So I saw you and that girl run off into the woods together, like a couple of teenagers."

It hit me like a ton of bricks: Greg knew everything. Maybe not the specifics, but he knew enough. He could easily surmise that we had kissed; otherwise I wouldn't have said so little about it. Greg scanned me up and down, glaring like I was his sworn enemy. I couldn't say anything.

"Have you talked to her since?" he asked.

"No." My answer was so quick and stern that there was no mistaking its authenticity.

"Good," he said. "You need to keep it that way. I get that you met some beautiful manic-pixie dream girl who is the answer to all of your problems, but she's more trouble than she's worth. She is thousands of miles away, and she probably has a boyfriend. Just like you"—he pointed at Carrie, who was laughing with her friends at the other end of the room"—have *her*."

I slapped his hand, pushing it down. "Damnit Greg," I said, "you don't think I realize what I did was wrong? I feel guilty enough as it is, without you constantly reminding me of what happened. I don't need your goddamn public service announcement. I know what I did."

I looked down. My second glass of wine was somehow already empty. I ferociously grabbed the bottle and poured its remaining contents into my glass. The wine wasn't the only thing swishing around; just from a couple small movements, I could tell that my body was beginning to feel slightly woozy. I shouldn't have been surprised that only two glasses of wine could hit my bloodstream so quickly, given how little I'd drunk over the past couple months. Carrie and I generally spent our time together watching movies as opposed to partying.

"Already on your second bottle, boys?" a voice suddenly asked. I hadn't noticed Carrie's return.

"Anna—" I began, when suddenly Greg's elbow hit me square in my ribcage, lightly knocking me to the side and causing me to nearly dump my wine on Carrie in the process. Only a millisecond had separated Greg's jab with my actually saying Annabelle's full name. The wine started to rise from my stomach, and my throat started to burn, almost like I was going to vomit. Carrie looked at me oddly. She couldn't have heard me, could she? Would it seem plausible that I was referring to another Anna at the party? I looked pleadingly toward Greg, who was staring angrily into his wineglass, unwilling to meet my eyes.

"Ladies and gentlemen!" Jake, our host, leapt up onto a chair, breaking the awkward tension. "I want to thank you all for coming tonight to my farewell party. Is everyone having a good time?"

The crowd erupted into a roar of applause, Greg included. Carrie clapped, too, but I remained still, stunned that my best friend had saved me from having to concoct stories about who the hell Annabelle was, and why her name had come up the moment Carrie arrived. As pissed off as I was with Greg's condescension toward my future outlook, I wanted to hug the man for preventing that calamity.

"Look," Jake continued, "all this cheese and wine bullshit is pretty cool and all, and I'm sure that in a few months when we're drinking on yachts and partying with the elites of the world, this will all be perfectly normal behavior." He paused, then dropped his wine glass on the floor right on his white carpet. We all gasped, but didn't notice until after the glass hit the floor that it was empty. He then opened up the flaps of his suit coat, revealing several sixteen-ounce cans of beer on the inside of the pockets.

"But you know what? We're not there yet! We still have two fucking weeks left of doing nothing, living life with no responsibilities, and sure as hell no jobs! So let's have some fun the good old fashioned way!"

He jumped off the chair at the exact same second that three other guys burst through the balcony doors with a giant keg. Watching Jake's display of grandeur pulled me from my funk, as I had no choice but to admire his antics. I also wondered if he had staged the entire party just so he could pull off this dramatic performance, or if the students at our school could only tolerate the idea of adulthood for so long before they demanded a keg.

The night shifted course from then on out. Mozart was replaced with hip-hop and loud rock music, and the volume was cranked to the stereo's highest audible levels. Most of the wine glasses disappeared from sight (though I did notice a few filled with beer) and were replaced with plastic cups. But most importantly, the conversations of careers, futures, and jobs that had dominated the earlier part of the party vanished. Greg and Jake argued over what baseball teams were hot this year, and I overheard Carrie and Stacey talking about the latest Top 40 songs. I mostly kept to myself, still a bit angry with Greg, despite his saving my ass earlier. I spoke little, choosing to be the only person continuing to consume wine instead of beer at this point, since it generated a certain type of drunk—a much looser one— that I hadn't felt before.

I glanced at my watch; the three of us had been socializing for nearly three hours, and the eighth glass of wine I had just finished (I still kept track) felt like a kick in the ass. Greg was undoubtedly more shitfaced than me or Carrie though, and even with my strong buzz, I noticed he was forced to lean up against a wall to keep his balance. I offered little assistance, almost relishing the fact that Greg couldn't hold his own at the grownup party he seemed to be so prepared for earlier.

"Should we go?" Carrie asked, motioning toward the door. She began to walk, and Greg and I followed. Walking behind her, I stared at her ass, which shook with zeal in that blue dress. Thankfully, the journey back to our apartment was only a couple hundred feet, but I never took my eye off of her body the entire walk. Once inside, a feeling of bliss ran through me the second I finally took off my shoes. Greg stumbled past the two of us, entering his room with a loud thud on the bed. The mattress springs squeaked, and within seconds any movement from that bedroom ceased. Carrie began to gather up her makeup she left earlier.

"Are you all situated here?" Carrie asked. "I'm going to

take off. Busy morning tomorrow."

"No," I said, reaching out and touching her leg. I found myself stroking her thigh, something I don't think I'd ever done before. "Please stay."

She appeared indifferent; I'm sure that a drunk version of her boyfriend was the last person she wanted to fool around with. Still, I persisted, rubbing her leg more, increasing the intensity with each stroke. My stroke eventually morphed into a squeeze, as Carrie let her head fall forward, her eyes closed, now staring down at the floor. To me, dropping her head confirmed her willingness to move forward, so I stood up and whisked her off the ground. I carried her into the bedroom and tossed her onto the bed.

Once on the bed, Carrie reopened her eyes and I could see the uncertainty plastered across her face. This type of aggression with Carrie was entirely new for me. She was the fourth girl I had ever had sex with, but I knew I was Carrie's second, which in itself laid a series of expectations upon me from our first night of intimacy. She liked being treated like a princess, preferring soft and delicate touches to the animal-like lust you'd often see in intense erotic thrillers. I also fell into that same camp, but only with Carrie did I have the opportunity to explore and try new things, the other three girls having been nothing more than random hookups that didn't last more than a couple weeks.

"Jass, do you—" she began, but I put my finger on her lips, stopping her. I didn't respond verbally, using only my body language to show her that tonight was going to be different. I flipped her body around and began to unzip her cocktail dress. It slid off with ease, and I tossed it on the floor. I began to kiss her neck, hard. I removed her bra and underwear, but I left my clothes on, waiting for her to rip them off on her own. And while she eventually did, tossing them to the floor on top of her dress, she did so gently and carefully, without the same intensity.

I continued on, touching Carrie in ways I never had before. She let me of course, but there didn't seem to be any enjoyment in her responses. Still, the alcohol blinded me to any feelings of indifference or disgust. And the moment we finished, I let out a big sigh. Something changed in me, but I wasn't sure what.

Carrie drifted off to sleep shortly after. For a while, I had trouble breathing, my heart racing and my breaths shortened. Plus the wooziness still hung around. But even when I regained composure, a simple fact remained: no matter how hard I had tried not to, the only girl I had pictured during sex was Annabelle.

****

Dear readers:

Well, well, well—it looks like I struck a cyber nerve with some of you guys in my Konacks recap from last week. I've posted at least six entries on different film, music and art happenings in the Portland area since, but the emails that keep filtering in mainly seem to concern my encounter with the mystery man, Jass. Most of the messages I have received are full of curiosity and legitimate questions; only a few were of the 'wtf' variety, as some of my male readers were confused—if not outright disappointed—about why I was wasting any cyberspace on non-artsy activities. Since I am a proponent of full disclosure as well as saving time (remember folks: time saved is time well spent), I thought that rather than respond to your emails individually, I'd address the frequently asked questions right here in this blog post:

Q: What did Jasper look like?
A: Tall, dark hair, handsome. But not sexy, at least not in the traditional sense.

Q: Is his name really Jasper?
A: Yes. He could have been lying, though he had an honest face. But not a sexy one. See previous question.

Q: I think I saw some hot short-haired chick at the concert making out with some dude. Was that you?
A: Not likely. I saw at least 17 people making out that night. And yes, I stopped counting at 17.

Q: Did you get a picture with him?
A: No, but I wish I had. Neither of us had cameras, and I figured a phone photo wouldn't do us justice.

Q: I'm a private investigator working at _____. Want me to help you find him?
A: No, that's super creepy. WTF are you doing reading my blog anyways? Do private investigators really care that much about Portland culture?

Q: You slept with him, didn't you?
A: You wish. I wish. We both wish.

Q: Do you believe in love at first sight? Did you fall in love with Jasper?
A: To the first question, no. That's a tired cliché. To the second question, no as well. But that's the thing—of course I didn't fall in love with Jasper after spending a few hours with him. That's not the point. The point is that, had we had more time together, we may have fallen in love someday. That's the type of attraction this was: it wasn't just a physical attraction between two individuals—it was the acknowledgement that there was something in the cosmos working in our favor, bringing us together. I think that's what people actually mean when they say they felt love at first sight.

I think that does it for the question and answer session, folks. It's been fun revisiting my Jasper encounter, though I think the journey with my mystery man has just about come to a close. It's been eight days since the concert, and while I will always look back on that night with a smile, I have to put it behind me. And so do you! Come on guys and gals, didn't you read my latest review of The Mason's new album? You should be listening to that gold token of a CD and not worrying about my (mis)fortune with the opposite sex.

With love,

Miss Mezzanine

# 3

The next Monday, Tundra hosted its spring semester career fair. The setup is fairly routine; you basically walk down a series of rows in a gymnasium, awkwardly smiling and buttering up recruiters from hundreds of different businesses who traveled to campus to scout out the latest and greatest talent. I considered career fairs exercises in futility, and had only ever gone to the previous ones for the plastic bags full of free shit: pens, magnets and key chains, most of which never made it all the way home.

Earlier at my apartment, Carrie scolded me for not wanting to go. She knew about the potential job at my dad's company, but I hadn't briefed her on my latest conversation with him. To her, it was still just a possibility, nothing more.

"Not going to a job fair is passing up free press for yourself," she said.

"Please Carrie," I responded. "Dedicating an hour to job searching on the internet probably has more positive results than spending an entire day speaking to anonymous recruiters you'll never see again."

"Whatever." Carrie waved away my argument. "Just go

for an hour with me."

Despite complaining about the validity and value of the job fair, the more accurate reason for my resistance was that I felt I had little to offer potential recruiters. I never took an internship, and my only experience with any on-campus jobs consisted of nothing more than taking papers from pile A and moving them to pile B. Acting never came naturally to me, so any line of questioning about my background would likely shed light on my lack of experience.

Finally, after more back-and-forth, I agreed to go, not because I was convinced my time would be well spent, but because Greg's tirade from Saturday still resonated with me, so if nothing else, I wanted to prove him wrong, that I didn't take everything thrown at me for granted.

Therefore, I was tremendously annoyed when, as I was en route to the fair, Carrie called and cancelled on me. She was stuck late in a study session but urged me to go without her. In the back of my head, I wondered if this hadn't been her plan all along, since she knew I wouldn't have bothered showing up on my own. Still, I had already dressed up and was literally standing next to the gym. Plus, if I didn't attend, that would mean having no options other than the position at my father's firm, and an inkling in my brain convinced me to keep my options open. I shut my phone and headed to the front doors.

When I walked in, there was a student ambassador at the entranceway to greet me: one of those overachievers responsible for coordinating every non-entertaining event on campus. Perkiness must have been the only job requirement; nearly every ambassador I'd ever encountered annoyed the hell out of me. Smiling, she handed me a giant Tundra-branded plastic bag.

"Enjoy!"

Enjoy? Clearly she possessed a misguided sense of entertainment.

The fair hours had just begun, so the giant room was

still fairly empty. There seemed to be more recruiters than recruitees, which put me in an awkward position: it would be especially difficult to bypass some of those B- and C-level employers if they weren't busy engaging with other students. I didn't want to look rude. Then again, I did have *some* sympathy for these people; their job required them to sit in a giant fluorescent-lit mega sized gym for five or six hours and to speak to every burnout, below-average philosophy major that came their way. And what was worse, they had to smile and nod as if the underachievers actually stood a chance at working for their organization.

Staring at the first row of exhibitors, I couldn't determine any sense of organization; there were at least a dozen different industries represented: finance, health, government, education, trade crafts, everything. Maybe it was Tundra's way of keeping the competition separate from one another. Or maybe it was just poor planning.

"You look lost," a voice said. I turned around. A young, suave-looking guy with slicked black hair stood at the booth, in front of a bright red table-clothed folding table by himself. He wore a black suit coat on top of a dark blue dress shirt, his tie a glossy solid black to match his hair. I looked at the name on the table cover: Rydel Media.

"More like disillusioned," I replied under my breath. I approached his table, eyeing up some of the free toys. I selected a bottle opener and a beer koozie.

"You guys really tailor your giveaways, huh?" I asked.

"We're great marketers," he laughed. He twirled his finger around, aiming at the ceiling. "It's like surrounding our booth with a bunch of bright shiny lights. Attracts lots of attention." He extended his hand, and I shook it. "I'm Ryan Felton."

"Jass Dietrich."

"Junior? Senior?"

"Senior."

"Ahh, the final few weeks of senior year." Ryan crossed

his arms and leaned against the table. "The last few weeks here for me were a total blur. I probably skipped half my classes and slept through the rest."

I did a double take. "Wait, you went to Tundra?"

"Yep." He nodded. "Class of 2000. Man, I really miss it here. Good to be back in my old stomping grounds again."

Tundra was small—maybe two thousand students in total—so I was surprised I didn't recognize him, even if he was a few years older. Greg and I had both been friends with upperclassmen, but neither Ryan's name nor his face rang a bell.

I pointed to the table cover. "What's Rydel Media?"

"It's a communications agency," he said. "Design work, marketing, advertising, all that jazz. Let me guess, you're a business major, right?" I thought of Annabelle saying the same thing. Apparently my degree was tattooed on my face. I nodded.

"Awesome, me too."

I couldn't think of anything else to add, since I had zero interest in the actual business he was representing. I had never heard of Rydel Media; it was likely a small firm tucked away in the bowels of northwestern Pennsylvania. Nowhere up my alley.

"Did you take Mr. Lester's Business in Politics class?" he asked. "Damn near failed the final exam. He's the only professor on the entire campus, I think, who has—"

"A through E on multiple choice," I interrupted. "I know. The trick to passing his tests was quickly figuring out that he favored A and E over the other letters. Once you went in with that mindset, it was easy to coast by with a B minus."

Ryan laughed and gazed off into space, likely recalling happy memories of drunken parties and one night stands. His nostalgic reverie didn't last long, though; the noise in the room was increasing with every second that passed. The poor ambassador was overwhelmed trying to hand out free bags to the hordes of students pouring through the doors.

I figured that Ryan Felton would want to gussy up his pitch for the next wave of students, rather than reminisce with someone who was clearly not his target audience. So I made the first move, doing the awkward thumb gesture toward the other side of the room. Ryan grabbed a business card from his pocket and handed it to me.

"Hey listen, take my card." He paused and looked at his watch. "If you're ever up in New York City, swing by." We shook hands again.

"New York City?"

"Yeah, Rydel Media's in Manhattan."

Annabelle's words immediately jumped into my mind.

*New York, where great artists are born.*

Pocketing his business card, I thanked him again and walked away, right after setting a copy of my resume down on his table for good measure. After all, he had given me his card.

As I wandered back up the first row of mediocre employers, any remaining interest was waning. I placed the handful of resumes I had brought into my goodie bag and spent the next twenty minutes walking from booth to booth, collecting as many free items as possible. I think I snatched at least fifteen different colored toothbrushes before my trip was over. On the dental hygiene front, I was set for life.

When I left the gym, I took a detour to a nearby student lounge on the third floor of the building, one of the few quiet places on campus that rarely received any traffic given its unique location. I took a few moments to sit on the room's only couch, the sound of the leather producing a quiet comforting puff when I hit the cushion. I stretched my legs, then pulled out Ryan's card and thought back to an exchange Annabelle and I had during the concert.

"I think I'm destined to end up in New York City," she declared. It was odd; she just finished bragging about her admiration for Portland's ascension to the music mecca of the country, and now she was idolizing New York. I pointed this out. "No," she told me, "great artists come to Portland, but they are born in New York City."

"What's so great about it?" I asked, repositioning myself on the blanket. I had never visited New York City, so all I really knew about it was that it had a lot of investment bankers and anything I might have picked up from popular sit-coms.

"It's hard to describe," she went on. Her enthusiasm was evident, as her hands did most of the talking for her. "But if you haven't experienced the city yourself, then you're definitely missing out. I spent five days in that city with my old roommate Kara, exploring the five boroughs, meeting people, tasting food. I made a point to try and stop in every café, every art gallery, and every music store that looked even remotely interesting." She glanced at me guiltily. "I promised I'd be sensible in my spending, but I must have bought about a hundred different items."

"You're kidding me."

"Nope," she said. "By the time I left New York City, I had emptied out my entire suitcase and replaced every possession I had brought with New York City memorabilia. Kara started calling me a walking gift shop. But I wear my badge proudly!"

God, that smile. And her way of always ending every story with some sort of life advice, even if she didn't set out to do so. I took one last glance at the New York address on Ryan Felton's business card and then tucked it away in my wallet. Before the next wave of seniors arrived, I snuck out through the back doors.

Carrie texted me a few hours later, wanting to grab some food. Her study session had ended, and she was just leaving the fair. I met her at The Shack, the only other cafeteria on campus that offered any food beyond vending machine items. She ordered a burger and fries, the good kind, where you end up consuming more grease than actual potato. Normally I would be snatching them off her plate, but I wasn't hungry.

"Any bites?" I asked. She stared at her hamburger questioningly, her mouth full of food. "At the fair, not the burger."

She laughed and continued chewing. "Some," she replied. "They all have my resume, and I'll probably send a few follow-up emails tonight. Maybe I'll get a response or two, who knows."

Carrie had more prospects than the average graduating senior, given her accomplishments, which were many. She was a health services major, and Pittsburgh was on the cutting-edge when it came to medical facilities, so she made sure to remind me time and time again how glad she was that she already lived in the right city. Excelling with a health services degree would likely earn her a spot at any number of hospitals in the area. And since both her immediate and extended families lived within a ten-mile radius of her home back in Pittsburgh, she didn't have the slightest interest in venturing beyond our hometown.

I told her I was proud of her.

"How about you? Make any good contacts?" she asked.

"None worth thinking twice about," I lied. I didn't want to tell her about Ryan Felton or Rydel. Even mentioning a company outside of Pittsburgh would likely set off a blaring alarm in Carrie's mind.

"Well that's ok," she replied, "I'm sure you'll get a few calls, anyway. As long as you dropped off your resume." I didn't have the heart to tell her that I only dropped off one, and that I was never going to get a call. She lowered her half-eaten burger and stared down at the plate.

"I want to be secure, Jasper." Her enthusiasm from earlier had suddenly vanished.

"We all do."

"No, most people want to be rich, famous, and highly successful, but that's not what I'm talking about." She looked around, as if to make sure no one was listening. "I'm not looking to score some fancy Corvette and a three-story Victorian home."

"And that's great. You're not greedy."

"My starter home can be my lifer home," she went on. "I don't care. Give me a dog and a garden, and I'll be happy, really." It was surprising to hear this coming from Carrie; I assumed her ambitions and overall approach toward her career meant always striving for the top and never settling for second best. "You're not scared at all, are you?"

"What do you mean, scared?" I asked. Was I supposed to be?

"We're about to be released into the wild with millions of other people, all trying to eat the same bread crumbs that the world leaves us. And we're all vultures. Everyone's anxious, stepping on top of one another to try and stand out. But over the last couple weeks, you've been coasting through, like you don't have a care in the world."

"I do care," I shot back. "Just because I'm not selling college prom tickets or spending every waking minute dusting off resumes and writing cover letters doesn't mean I haven't been thinking about what's going to happen to me after I graduate."

"Me?" she asked. "Not us? Do you realize how hard it is to look for jobs, to plan for my next steps, when you're not doing the same? I don't know whether to look north, south, east, west…. No idea where I want to live, whether I should look be looking at apartments or houses. Pittsburgh is a big city, Jass."

"What's the point, Carrie?" I asked. I was quickly becoming irritated. I thought of my father and his lecture on my lack of focus. "None of us end up with what we truly want anyway, so what's the point in worrying? Just let things play out."

"I don't get you, Jass," she said, her disappointment glaring in every word. "I don't know whether or not I'm jealous or concerned. I keep going back and forth." She glanced at her watch. "Look, I have to go. I have to study." She said goodbye, threw away half of her food, and was out of the cafeteria before I could even respond.

It didn't take a detective to realize she felt betrayed by my words, and in an instant I felt another brick of guilt shock through my chest. Carrie never cried, at least not in front of me, but the pure disappointment expressed on her face was far worse than tears. I could only imagine how she'd look at me if she knew everything.

And what would Annabelle think? About this? About Carrie? Annabelle, the charming independent woman that she was, would likely have ended our conversation with a handshake and farewell on that blanket if she had known that Carrie even existed.

But I knew what Annabelle would think about Ryan Felton. "If you don't grab what's in front of you, someone else always will," she had said at one point that night. She would probably be pushing me out the cafeteria doors, insisting that I catch Ryan again before he left campus, which was likely soon. The fair ended at six o'clock, and my watch read about quarter till. Ryan had probably met a hundred other students who had made better impressions on him, but our conversation had ended so abruptly that I felt I needed to try again, regardless of where it took me. So I went.

When I returned to the gymnasium a few minutes later, most of the companies had already cleared out, so it was easy to spot Ryan Felton, who, unlike the others, was taking his time gathering all of his items. I approached him as he was rolling up the Rydel Media tabletop.

"Jass!" he exclaimed. "Welcome back." He didn't look surprised to see me. I pointed at the empty table.

"I see you got cleaned out of all your little goodies."

"Us Tundra Titans love our booze. I'm actually surprised they let us give those things away. Probably promotes unruly behavior." He finished shoving the rest of his materials into a giant bag and slung everything over his shoulder. "What brings you back?"

"I just realized that I didn't really get a chance to learn more about your company," I responded. "Thought maybe we could catch up a little more, and you could fill me in."

"Sure!" he said, with no hesitation. "Let me just run this out to my car, and we can take a walk. Millers is still here, right?" He laughed. "They didn't tear the place down or anything, did they?"

"No, still open," I laughed. Asking me to accompany him to a bar wasn't quite what I had expected; I had assumed we would talk for a little more near the gym. But something about his presence put me at ease. Maybe it was the fact that he was a Tundra alumnus, or his generally enthusiastic demeanor, but I was actually looking forward to going.

I followed him to his car, where he loaded in his gear, and then we began the walk toward Millers. During the walk I watched him closely. He appeared so confident, so enamored with the college that he spent the entire walk talking about the things and people (mostly girls) that he missed the most. What could have easily been a five-minute walk took almost fifteen minutes, since Ryan purposely took every detour in order to visit some of the campus hot spots: the football field, the playhouse, the library, the brook.

When we finally arrived at the bar, swarms of students blocked nearly every available table. Millers was the Cheers of the Tundra community, the homey place that attracted the same people day in and day out. I remembered having a couple drinks there for my twenty-first birthday party last year, but it wasn't a place that I frequented. Why, when everyone lived within walking distance of each other, did people prefer to leave campus to drink at a loud, expensive, dimly lit hovel where there was no room to breathe? Still, Millers did have one perk going for them: their wing dings were legendary.

The hostess managed to seat us at the one remaining two-seater at the very back of the bar, handed us each a menu, and was gone again before either of us could ask for a drink. I looked at Ryan, and though I was just two years younger than him, I felt like a pre-schooler in the presence of the prom king.

"I bet you don't often grab wings and beer with people you meet at job fairs," I joked nervously.

"Nah," he replied, "and that's probably because it's the first time I've ever done one of these."

"You're not a recruiter?"

"Noooo." He shook his head violently. "Our main HR person was sick. I'm just an account executive who volunteered to visit his alma mater."

The waitress finally appeared, and Ryan ordered a beer. I was incredibly thirsty, but I was afraid of looking foolish by just drinking water and not ordering alcohol like he had. So I ordered the same beer. She asked if we were ready to order food. I hadn't even looked at the menu, but it was an act of blasphemy to eat anything other than the wing dings, so we each ordered a dozen.

"So, account executive—is that just a fancy way of saying you're in sales?"

He nodded and smiled, like I had cracked a secret code.

The waitress returned with our beers. Ryan took a big swig. "I might be a sales rep, but trust me, I'm not trying to sell you anything. You'll get enough of that in your life, especially right after you graduate. I did happen to look at your resume a little bit after you left. You look like a guy who has a good head on his shoulders. God love this place, but so many people here seem to have no direction, no vision."

His first impression radar must have burnt a fuse. If only he had been sitting beside Carrie an hour ago, or at the party with Greg the other night. They could have given each other high fives as they enlightened him on my lack of focus for my future.

"Well, I'm not sure my resume was *that* clear cut."

"Good grades, a couple jobs on campus. I'm surprised you're still searching for a job at all. Nothing stick yet?"

"Nah, not yet."

Our conversation came to a screeching halt. I felt like he was waiting for me to say something, to ask questions about him or his company, anything to keep the conversation going, but I was drawing a blank. I started to think about that night at the concert, how it had been so easy to come up with things to say to Annabelle, who had—like Ryan— been a complete stranger. And though I liked Ryan, and he seemed like a generally honest person, he was looking for a part of me that didn't seem to exist.

As the silence lingered, his eyes started to drift to a pair of young girls at the other end of the bar.

"So many good times here, Jass," Ryan said, his eyes still glued to the girls. "There's not a day that goes by that I don't think about this place and my four years here. Probably the best time of my life."

"Is there anything you would change?" I asked.

"Not one thing," he said, and then paused. "I guess I wish I would have seen the light quicker than I did, but that's part of the learning process."

"Seen the light?" This guy wasn't going to start preaching religion, was he?

"I just wasted so much time going through life walking on eggshells. Putting myself second, or even worse, last. The trick is to just ignore all the distractions and do what's best for you. The rest falls into place."

"Did you practice that on the way over here?" I nearly

rolled my eyes. "That sounds a little bit too Ayn Rand-ian to me."

"No, no, no, this isn't being selfish," he pushed back. "It's about making sure you have the energy and the commitment to do what you need to do. And that's what I meant when I said so many people lack vision."

Despite Ryan's inclination to be a bit in the clouds with his preachiness, I must admit there was something intriguing about how he was presenting himself. Maybe he was in fact this over-confident, highly philosophical guy who was guided by this sort of moral compass. Or maybe he was just a snake oil salesman, gearing up for the ultimate pitch. Either way, his self-confidence was refreshing, especially in his diagnosis of college seniors. Even Greg and Carrie, definitely people who were goal-oriented, seemed to approach graduating (and life in general) by looking for ways to stay afloat as opposed to ways to stand out.

"Yeah, everyone's too focused on where they're going to land in the pit when they should be thinking about how to climb out," I said, speaking metaphorically, hoping to impress.

"Exactly!" Ryan beamed.

"Not many people are as pessimistic as you are, that's for sure," I noted, taking another sip from my beer.

Ryan laughed. "If anything, I'm the most optimistic person you'll ever meet."

"I guess I would be, too, if I was living high and mighty in New York City. How is it living there?"

Ryan leaned back in his chair. He placed his hands behind his head, thinking. "It's interesting," he responded. "There's something for everybody. I'm always finding new things to do and places to see. But it's just a place, and Rydel is just a job. Not the first one or the last one I'll have. It's a stepping stone. A stepping stone that pays well."

I thought back to Annabelle. *In New York, I felt free Jass*, she had said. I pictured her walking down Fifth Avenue, a backpack saddled on her shoulders, staring at all of the buildings and snapping pictures on her camera at every corner. Annabelle was shocked I had never visited, and said that everyone owed it to themselves to visit once, if even only to say they had stepped foot in one of the world's largest cities. My favorite statement of hers was, *There have to be more exciting places than Pittsburgh, right?*

"Let me ask you something," Ryan said, pulling me out of my daze. "Say you graduate tomorrow and were offered a job in New York. Good starting salary, great benefits, three weeks vacation. But you have to start in two days. What would you say?"

What else could I do but laugh? Hypothetical situations are meaningless, especially one as implausible as this one. But since Ryan was most likely buying the wing dings that had finally made their way back to our table, I decided to play along.

"Well, a few things would be problematic. For one, I wouldn't have a place to—"

"You could sublet for a few months until you found something more permanent," he shot back before I could finish.

"Well I have a home—"

"I doubt you have a mortgage."

I hesitated saying the third reason, and though Ryan knew nothing of my personal life, he could read it on my face.

"Let me guess. Girlfriend?"

Down goes Frazier. Not only would Carrie be reluctant to move, she would refuse. Anything outside of Pittsburgh was out of the cards. Plus, she had been to New York once and equated the city to a public bus with standing room only, filled with smelly people packed like sardines.

But why was I even thinking about Carrie's reaction? This was nothing but a charade—just table conversation with someone who was enjoying his position of power and influence. Nothing more.

"She wouldn't go for it," I said. "Not this girl, anyway." It wasn't until a few seconds had passed that I realized I had indirectly inferred that there was *another* girl who would be willing to make that leap with me. But she wasn't here.

"Ah," he said, "it always comes down to the girlfriend. Seen it a million times."

"You know," I began, but stopped. The next few thoughts that entered my mind were dangerous ones, ones that I knew if spoken aloud would become permanent and undeniable. But they needed to be said, even if I would regret them. "Even a few days ago, I felt like there was no stopping this train that was coming right at me."

"A train wreck?" he asked.

"Not a train *wreck*," I continued. "Just a train. A train of predictability. It's like I'm standing right there on the tracks, staring at this massive heap of expectations coming my way, a thousand miles an hour. And I can either stand still on the tracks, and let this train pick me up—which would determine the course for the rest of my life: with my career, with Carrie, a mortgage, kids"—I hesitated, realizing that Ryan had no idea who Carrie was, but he seemed to pick up on it—"or, I could take two steps to the left, and let the train pass me by.

"It's not really that difficult, just two steps. But those two steps would change the entire trajectory of my life. The train would keep going wherever it was going without me. And once that train passed, it would be impossible for me to ever hop back on, and I'd have to figure out where else to go, what else to do.

"I've thought about this train for a while, and every day I can feel it coming a little bit closer. Then, a couple weeks ago, for the first time ever, I met someone who actually urged me to take those two steps off the track."

"And your girlfriend? Is she on this train that is coming to ruin your life?"

"Yes. No. I mean, this has nothing to do with her. She can do anything she wants with her life. But she hasn't jumped at anything yet, because she's waiting for me to make the first move. And that scares me. I don't want to have the burden of someone else's life on my shoulders. I'm not ready for that."

I stopped, horrified at how many of my random thoughts had spilled out on full display for this stranger. For all I knew the guy was engaged or in a committed relationship, which meant that he would probably dismiss me outright for taking my girlfriend for granted. But he didn't budge.

"Believe it or not, I've been there," he responded.

My eyebrows instinctively raised. "Really?"

"Yeah," he went on, "the girl I dated since we were fifteen. High school sweethearts. Turned into college sweethearts. Didn't realize we were well past our expiration date until after we both graduated. Then a buddy of mine moved to New York City and kept urging me to follow him. So it came down to a choice."

"What happened?"

He opened his arms, looking down at the empty space between them. "You don't see anyone with me, do you?" I thought about pummeling him with another barrage of questions, to learn if his relationship bore any resemblance to ours. But then another thought immediately jumped to mind.

"Wait a minute. On the way here, you kept talking about all those girls you were with at Tundra."

He shrugged his shoulders. "I'm not perfect, Jass," he responded, "and maybe that's another reason why Erica and I never stood a chance." He paused, biting off a chunk of meat from his last wing ding. "Look, there's a position about to open up at my company, which basically consists of business analytics stuff. We need someone who's good with numbers but who also has some creativity, can strategize a bit, all that jazz. They're going to be looking for college graduates, but ones who aren't demanding outrageous salaries. And I'm not making any promises or anything, but I could probably get you an interview. Might be one of your two steps."

I was stuttering a bit, trying to find the right words, when the waitress came over to drop off the check. My scattered thought process was interrupted even further when Ryan stood up before I could articulate anything coherent. He grabbed the check from the center of the table before I had a chance to reach for it, pulled out two twenty dollar bills, and placed them inside the check.

"Listen, I have to hit the road now if I want to get back before midnight, but think everything over. Do some research; figure out what you works for you. You have my card, so you know how to find me. Ok?"

I thanked him for dinner at least five times, but he kept insisting it was no problem. We exchanged our goodbyes, and he reiterated that I should stay in touch. Once he left, I sat there on my own to finish my beer, looking at his business card again and wanting to rip the thing up and leave the pieces in the pile of barbeque sauce on my plate. Not out of anger, but because it was an implausible temptation, one that in the end would likely lead to disappointment. I didn't want to go down that road. Ultimately, though, my curiosity won out, saving the business card from a barbeque-sauce-covered fate just as the waitress came over to collect the check.

"Everything turn out ok?" she asked, gathering the empty plates from the table and piling them up on her large tray.

"That's a good question." I twirled Ryan's card around in my fingers. "I'm not sure yet."

\*\*\*\*

Dear readers:

When it comes to blogging, the only thing standing between your mind vomit and hundreds of readers is your ability to self-edit. And unfortunately, most bloggers fail to undergo this important self-editing process; they disregard their audience, spew a bunch of nonsense, click "publish," and wait for the hits to pour in.

One rule of thumb for my blogging friends (and I say this with the utmost respect): write your blog post, leave your computer, and do whatever it is you need to do to stay away for at least an hour—run a few miles, bake a cake, do some laundry, whatever. When you return to your computer, re-read your blog, and still find it interesting, THEN and ONLY THEN hit "publish." I'm a huge fan of this method; every blog post stamped with the Mezzanine seal of approval sits on hold while I watch a cartoon, take a nap, or form a posse before I return and stamp it "approved." However, tonight I am breaking my rule because I must vent, and in an hour I hope to be drowning myself in booze.

Earlier this week, I met up with a college friend for coffee, and she somehow convinced me to go on a blind date with her co-worker, a young guy who was allegedly a Casanova type and very 'philosophical'. Those two qualities aren't necessarily ones I look for in the Perfect Man, but my friend (and I know you're reading this, dear; the next coffee we have together I am spiking with ex-lax) gave him a strong recommendation. And since I haven't been on a real date in months, I went out on a limb and accepted. A breakdown of the night's events:

1. Can't Take a Hint. Guy arrives at girl's apartment to pick her up. Apartment is an absolute atrocity, so girl tells guy over the phone she'll meet him outside. Guy ignores request and knocks on girl's door anyway. Girl panics when she hears knock, opens door, and proceeds with awkward introduction through three-inch crevice. Guy insists on coming inside anyway. Girl gives guy panoramic view from hallway, jokes that place is a mess, and speeds out the door. Girl thanks God guy did not see kitchen.

2. First Base Only. Within five minutes of small-talk en route to restaurant, guy casually drops the word 'tits'. Girl feels boobs probably shouldn't be a topic of discussion during a first date. However, if they must be mentioned, more respectful vernacular from guy would be appreciated.

3. Not Over It. Throughout dinner, guy mentions ex-girlfriend ("Brandy") at least four times. That doesn't particularly bother girl—previous relationships will always be a part of natural growth— but each mention seems more endearing than the last. When the ex's name is said more than your own during dinner, that's usually a red flag.

4. Men are From Mars. Guy lacks general sense of situational awareness and unintentionally criticizes girl's opinions on various topics. This leads girl to refrain from divulging certain details about herself (this blog among them) for fear of somehow being mocked. Guy—while certainly witty—also tends to inject humor in certain discussions that don't quite require it. Nothing like cracking an offensive joke when talking about geopolitics.

5. Going Home Alone. Despite C+ dinner and movie, girl permits a kiss on the cheek out of pure kindness. Apparently guy interprets kiss on cheek as "let's get busy," as guy suggests not once, not twice, but three times that girl

has nightcap at guy's place. Guy even called it the 'love cabin'. Downgraded to an "F".

Granted, I'm overstating a bit when I say it was horrible. The main takeaway was that throughout dinner, my mind drifted off, and I kept wondering what a traditional first date would have been like with Jasper. I imagine he would have been chivalrous, but not patronizing. I also think that Jasper would have preferred to do something physical (not that, hardy-har-har), like a quiet walk through an art gallery or miniature golf. But I am certain that he would have posed questions to elicit answers he really wanted to hear, not just to serve as a bridge between picking a girl up and getting laid. Sadly though, Jasper isn't around to prove me right, so I'm stuck here thinking of a way to politely refuse when wannabee John Locke surely asks me out on a second date.

Any good tips?

Miss Mezzanine

# 4

After Ryan Felton's abrupt exit, I immediately snuck back to my apartment to lie down. Despite feeling as if Ryan and I had spent the entire evening together, by the time I returned it was only eight o'clock. I wasn't sure which of the three components of the day had worn me out the most: the fair, my argument with Carrie, or the dinner. My phone sat dormant throughout dinner, but it didn't matter; I knew there weren't any messages waiting for me. Carrie's preferred method of fighting consisted of either shutting off communication completely or flavoring every ounce of conversation with sarcasm.

Just as I was finished getting changed into my green-checkered flannel pants and long-sleeved bright crimson Tundra sweatshirt (my go-to "comfy clothes" as I called them), Greg burst through my door. He was nearly out of breath, and even from a few feet away, the booze-filled stench was unmistakable.

"Celebrating Messy Monday a bit early tonight?" I watched his body sway back and forth in my doorway.

"Only a handful of them left Jass," he laughed. "You should . . . you should . . . be taking advantage like I am."

He pulled out my computer chair and sat down. "I ran into Carrie earlier, and she said you went to the fair. You already got your job, man. Don't be stealing any good leads from the rest of us minions."

"I thought you weren't going."

"Jass, haven't I taught you anything by now? If you're going to—" he stopped for a moment to belch "—put all your chips on red, at least save a few for the next spin. I'm strategizing Jass. Strategizing."

I could have brought him down to size by telling him what had transpired over the past six hours. Greg possessed a natural competitiveness with everyone (including me), and the fact that I had met with an inside guy for a one-on-one get-together (especially at a place like Millers) would have driven him crazy with envy. But given the open-endedness of our discussions, I didn't want to open up a can of worms to a line of questioning I wasn't prepared to address. So I kept my mouth shut.

"Now come on, let's go out and party." He urged me to come, waving his hand.

"Nah, I think I'm staying in tonight," I responded. I was sailing on some odd type of euphoria from earlier, wondering how Ryan was interpreting our evening on his drive back to New York City. I couldn't think about partaking in anything else right now, least of all a beer-drenched party.

"Well you enjoy the rest of your night," Greg said. "I'm going for some round twos. And remember, save a few of your chips for Tipsy Tuesday." Greg stumbled out of my room laughing, and I shut the door behind him.

Instead of going to bed early, as I had intended, I watched two different movies based in New York City. They both had that gritty undertone, shot in grainy stock film and on the shaky cameras—straight-to-DVD stuff. Not that film was a reputable source of research, but I liked to watch movies to learn more about different topics, and right now I wanted to learn more about New York City.

The conclusion of my research was that even though the city contained eight million people, everyone seemed to possess a sense of community and friendliness, so the city was almost like a sum of small villages. It stood in stark contrast to a place like Pittsburgh, where everyone seemed to keep to themselves. Even after spending my entire life there, never once did I detect that type of camaraderie with strangers (sans Steelers games, maybe). The last image I saw before falling asleep was that of the New York City skyline, with the old, towering World Trade Center glistening in the moonlight.

The next morning, as soon as I managed to shut off my blaring alarm clock, I noticed the screen of my phone was lit—it was a text message from Carrie. The message was clear and to the point:

*Don't want to fight. Meet me at Dark Roast after first class.*

To avoid any misunderstandings—my experience with girls was that they tended to try and read between lines you never even wrote—I simply responded with:

*Sounds great, see you at two.*

The moment I clicked 'send', I sighed: despite saying she didn't want to fight, Carrie might well change her tune depending how much I chose to disclose about the past twenty-four hours.

Heading to the bathroom to get ready, I nearly tripped over the empty DVD cases I had left on the floor the night before. However, where I normally would pick these up and make my room more orderly, for some reason today I just didn't care. It could wait. It could always wait.

Before I walked into McLaren Hall a few minutes later, I

overhead a faint cry around the corner. My general inclination would usually be to try and ignore it, so as to not intrude on anyone's personal business, but I couldn't shake the sadness in what I was hearing, especially since it conflicted with the overall sense of joy that I felt from last night's meeting with Ryan. Much to my surprise, as I rounded the corner, I actually recognized the girl sitting on the old wooden bench, knees clenched together, her tiny hands sticking out from her spring jacket, wiping tears and snot from her face. It was Stacey. Against my better judgment, I slowly approached, trying my best not to startle her.

"Stacey, what's wrong?"

She flinched when she noticed me, quickly wiping her entire face again. "It's umm . . . it's nothing," she said, sniffling between each of her words, "just not having the best of mornings."

Normally I'd be inclined to leave it at that, wish her a better day, and take off. We ordinarily maintained only a very basic level of a civility, and trying to comfort a person who sort of disliked me represented quite a challenge. Still, seeing her cry in the loneliest of spots, on an isolated side of a building, prompted me to ask myself what I would want in that situation. I'd want company. So, ignoring all of my other instincts, I took the open seat on the bench next to her.

"No sense in being modest," I said. "That's never been your style. Not toward me at least."

She laughed, or tried to anyway, emitting more of a light cough. "It's really nothing. I just found out Simpson Tech is spinning off their accounting department to somewhere in New Jersey." I didn't follow, which she must have realized pretty quickly. "I intern there now. They all but promised me a full-time job when I graduated. Now I have nothing."

"Oh no Stacey, I'm sorry. But it's really not that bad.

They're not the only company out there. Surely not the only one that needs accountants."

"Where am I going to go, Jass? Everyone else got a head start on me." She turned to me, eyeing me up and down. "And no one in my family can line up a job for me."

I tried my best to give her the benefit of the doubt with that statement—her meaning she had nowhere to fall back on versus criticizing me for my privileges—and focus on the larger point she was making. That a sure thing fell apart.

"Can I ask you something? Did you even like your internship? I mean, would you have fought for that job, applied even, had you not been interning?"

"Umm, probably not," she replied, "but it's accounting. There's no such thing as a dream accounting job. You take what you can get."

"Agreed," I went on, "but wouldn't you rather have this happen now, rather than months later, after you've already settled in your new life? Take it as a blessing, Stacey. If anything, you dodged a bullet."

"You think so?"

"I know so," I answered. "There will be plenty of things in life worth crying over. Some stupid tech company's accounting department should not be one of them."

She forced a smile, and I realized that I had exhausted all of my optimistic advice. Had this been Carrie, or any other friend or acquaintance of mine, I'd likely go in for the hug and tell them again that it's all going to be ok. But with Stacey, an unease still separated us, and despite my attempt at finding a silver lining in her situation, she likely took every word I said with a grain of salt. Maybe a few grains. So I only stood up and waved.

"I'll see you in class?" I asked.

"Yeah," she responded, "see you in class."

I turned around and headed back toward the building's entrance, catching a glimpse of Stacey out the corner of my eye as I turned the corner. She still sat on the bench, but she no longer cried. Maybe I had made an impact after all. Still, I pitied her. But most of all, I feared for myself. Feared that one day I'd be the one on the bench, crying over a missed opportunity that I had, in my ambivalence, simply allowed to pass me by.

Astonishingly, my first class, Advertising and Ethics, was not only less painful than usual, but somehow more interesting. The material itself was no different, but listening to someone talk about their experiences working outside of academia was, for the first time, fascinating. I thought about Ryan Felton, and how his confidence could easily carry a two-hour lecture to a room full of eager seniors. However, the audience he had chosen was just one: me. When the class was over, and everyone hustled out to their next lecture, I instead waited for Professor Lensing to finish gathering his notes. He was stunned when he saw me.

"Mr. Dietrich," he said, shutting his briefcase, "to what do I owe this pleasure?"

"Professor, can I ask you a question?" He nodded. "I feel like you've accomplished so much in your career. But have you ever wondered what it would be like to start things over? To take a different path?"

"Interesting question," he responded, "especially considering how little tenure you have left at this University. Short answer is no, Mr. Dietrich. I'm one to think that all of the big decisions we make—job, marriage, location—are all the ones we know we're supposed to make. It's usually the little ones we screw up and wish we could change. Hope that helps."

"It does," I responded, "thanks Professor."

Seconds later I took off down the hall and soon arrived at The Dark Roast, Tundra's only coffee shop on campus. As expected, the place was chock-full of underclassmen, faces hidden behind books, coffees balanced precariously on the armrests of chairs or squeezed into crevices of table space between computers, cramming for around-the-clock exams. As a senior with my own, more ample living (and studying) space, I didn't bother with the place much anymore. I preferred the comfort of my own bedroom rather than the small talk and over-amplified whispers that were all-too distracting here or in the library.

I spotted Carrie in the back corner, scribbling something in a notebook, her favorite mocha drink set in front of her. As I walked over, she caught me out of the corner of her eye and stood up. She waved to me with such enthusiasm that I thought her arms were going to rip right out of their sockets. She hugged me harder than she ever had and with such veracity that it was hard to believe she had had any negative feelings toward me earlier.

"You're so eager. What happened?" I asked. The smile on her face did not fade one bit as she pulled me to a nearby table.

"Pitt Med called me back this morning. They want me to come in for a second interview!" She slapped her hands on the table in joy, but then hesitated, as if my response might dictate whether her celebration would be allowed to continue. I tried to hide my confusion, since my immediate reaction was that I didn't recall her going in for a first interview. It only took a few seconds before I remembered that she had in fact made a comment about speaking with someone on the phone about a job opportunity at Pittsburgh's biggest medical center. It had been during spring break, a time that felt like a lifetime ago.

"That's great Carrie," I responded, knowing I couldn't ask many follow-up questions since I didn't remember much about the job in the first place. "So what are the next steps?"

"Well," she said, pulling a crumpled piece of paper out of her pocket. She unraveled it, and I recognized her scribbles of handwriting covering the paper, "they asked me when I was free, so I told them I could meet with them as early as Friday. Next week is probably easier, since it's the last week of classes, but I didn't want to risk them interviewing other people first. I read a statistic that first-interviewed candidates are chosen for positions over half of the time."

The news startled me, and I could barely move. Here I was, walking over to the coffee shop, trying to determine whether or not to tell Carrie about this mystery man and the mere *possibility* that an opportunity may be lurking in the mist, and she was one or two polite meetings away from landing a job at one of Pittsburgh's largest employers. I tried my best to ignore the irony.

"Wow. You should start readying up for this interview then. I'm sure it won't be a cakewalk."

I didn't know why it was so hard for me to feel immediate joy for Carrie—she was an incredibly hard worker and certainly deserved this opportunity more than anyone—but my first response was a sort of bitterness. Perhaps because her tangible prospect marked another step closer to solidifying her future and in the exact ways she hoped for. Or because everything that had happened to me was nothing more than a shot in the dark.

Carrie saw right through my forced congratulatory smile. She only nodded, clenching her teeth and taking another sip from her mocha. The loud suction through the straw was worse than an awkward silence, and I thought right then about leaving the table and ordering something for myself, just to get away if even for a moment. If only there were a way to reset this entire conversation, so I had time to prepare for what she was saying.

"Something happened in Portland, didn't it?" Carrie asked. Her voice was soft. Her earlier enthusiasm had instantly evaporated, and she wouldn't look at me, her body motionless—waiting. The words sliced right into me.

"No!"

That one word had so much power in its deceit, because nothing could have been further from the truth. But it was an instant reaction. 'Yes' would have taken an amount of courage I never would have been able to muster in such a short amount of time. I wanted to ask 'why', to know what had made her ask the question in the first place, but I was afraid of what she would say. Was it because I had entirely avoided sex since Jake's party? Because I've barely engaged her in anything beyond necessary conversations? There were so many potential answers that I couldn't bring myself to ask the question. I found myself hoping—praying—that she'd stand up and storm out of the coffee shop rather than ask me anything else.

"Ok. Because I hope you would save me the embarrassment of ever having to ask twice."

When she took another drink, that's when I knew she wouldn't pry anymore. But her statement made it clear: the ball was now in my court. I think she could tell something had happened, even if she didn't know the specifics, and the onus was on me to come forward on my own. While most guys would thank their lucky stars to be given this opportunity to 'get away with it', she was testing my true morality, and I knew right away that I wouldn't pass the exam.

We sat there, separated only by a tiny brown wooden table, our continued silence overrun by the chattering freshmen and pop music in the background. I wanted so desperately to tell her everything about that night in Portland. But I knew doing so would devastate her, and with only three days until she would go on the interview that could potentially land her a fantastic job in a high-tech medical facility, I couldn't interfere. However, I knew she still needed some acknowledgement that she wasn't imagining the changes in me. Without that, she would only continue to worry, to analyze, distracting her from everything else she needed to focus on.

"There is something I've been hiding from you." Before I even finished my sentence, she was shaking her head back and forth, clearly expecting me to confirm her suspicions.

"It's about the fair." She stopped shaking.

"The career fair? From yesterday? What about it?"

I told her about my initial meeting with Ryan. I told her how we spoke for about ten minutes, just friendly banter, and how he seemed to take an interest in me. I told her about Millers, and how for some reason still not fully known to me, I had decided to go with him. There were parts I left out, like Ryan's overall cockiness, which I doubt Carrie would appreciate. I certainly didn't mention how Ryan suggested, if not encouraged me, to leave Carrie behind and venture off into the wider world. But there was no way to avoid mentioning the fact that the sort of job he had sort of offered me was definitely in New York City.

"New York? Jass, why would you want to move to New York?"

"I didn't. I mean I don't. I doubt I'm even going to follow up with him. It was just an informal meeting with a guy I will likely never talk to again."

"Bullshit. How can I believe you right now? I was with you right after the fair and you completely hid this all from me."

"Carrie, please." I reached out to grab her hand.

"No Jass." She stopped me, pushing my hand away. "I'm leaving. I need to prep. Good luck with your job prospect." She stormed out of the coffee shop, turning a number of heads in the room, and for the third time in two days, I was left sitting by myself, abruptly abandoned.

When my final class of the day ended and I got back to my apartment, I barricaded myself in my bedroom, deciding to do a little more research on Rydel Media. The website was impressive, which I guess shouldn't have been a surprise given their focus in advertising and media. From the pictures on their homepage, I could see that their office was located near Central Park, which to my limited understanding was in Central Manhattan.

I continued to dig deeper, still not exactly sure of what I was looking for. The more I read, the more everything came alive, from the designs on each page, to their business goals. Even their 'careers' page, packed with mundane details about benefit packages and great working environments read like an interesting magazine article to me, since it predicated thoughts of actually having a salary and disposable income, something I've considerably lacked as a college student.

Maybe it was time to email Ryan back. Even without any idea of what to expect from our interactions, or whether or not I would actually apply for a job with his company, it still made sense to keep my options open. Right? Absenteeism would kill any chances of maintaining the connection, so even if it was just to say thanks for the wings, I had to write something.

I pulled out his business card, which had been securely stored in my top dresser drawer. I twirled the glossy card in my fingers as I stared at the blank white screen of my school email account. I typed the first sentence. Deleted it. Typed another sentence. Deleted that one too. Over and over I did this until finally my frustration peaked. I wanted to scream at my computer screen. Why was it so difficult to write what was supposed to be a very casual email? I kept including phrases like 'It was a pleasure getting to know you' or 'I'm deeply appreciative', cookie-cutter pleasantries that, based on the casualness and intimacy of our interaction, I simply could not say. Finally I stopped pretending to be an upper-class snob and wrote exactly what I wanted to say:

*Ryan, definitely interested in an opportunity. Just let me know what's next. —Jass.*

I hit 'send' before I had time to second-guess myself and then slammed my hands on my desk for dramatic effect. It was ridiculous that it had taken me half an hour to write a two-sentence email, when I had no way of knowing whether this guy would even be able to deliver on his word. After all, the guy had graduated college only two years ahead of me; how much influence could he possibly have? Maybe his visit to Tundra was nothing more than a chance to relive his former glory. He had readily admitted that he didn't even do recruiting for Rydel. Maybe I should have waited until I had something more concrete before I told Carrie about him. Because what was the point of enduring her wrath if this all just came to nothing, anyway?

Doubt flooded through me, and my head began to ache. I needed a break. Without even stopping to grab my jacket, I stormed out of my apartment and into the cool evening air. By now, the sky had begun to fade, its earlier brilliant blue hue turning a pale off-shade of lavender. I decided to follow a particular limestone trail, which stretched around the campus and led into the woods. Other than the students who lived in my apartment complex, few Tundra folks ever bothered to walk the path, which meant that it was often completely empty. That emptiness, the open road, was exactly what I needed.

As I crunched along the limestone trail, the surrounding silence amplified every sound within a hundred yards tenfold. For a little while, I only heard the occasional chirping of a bird, buzz of a cricket, and dry scrap of sticks scuttling across the ground each time I encountered one and kicked it out of my way. But soon the voices began echoing inside my head, louder and louder until I could no longer ignore them. First I heard Annabelle, describing the rock in the forest, and for a moment I thought I actually saw it appear right in front of me in the woods. Then I heard Greg, telling me to wake up, how the good-looking "distraction" I had met at the concert would ruin me.

Lastly, I heard myself talking to Carrie in the café, telling her about the possibility of a job in New York City. My voice was honest, my words sincere, but the whole time, I envisioned everything I was omitting piling up behind me, threatening to tumble down in an avalanche of lies. Telling her about Ryan Felton was a cop-out. It was the coward's way of telling her that maybe our perfectly planned future wasn't what I wanted anymore, that while I wasn't going to tell her what had happened in Portland, it was important enough to change my perspective on life, on her. Maybe Carrie had sensed all of this beneath my words, or maybe she was just tired of questioning things.

Just as I was exiting the other end of the trail, I noticed a figure walking toward me. The tiny amount of sunlight left cast a shadow, and after a few more steps I made him out: Greg. We were far enough away from the rest of campus that his heaving breaths amplified as he approached, like a fiery locomotive train gaining speed. He didn't stop walking until he stood inches from my face.

"Care to fill me in, Jass?"

My God, he was angry, huffing short, repetitive breaths in my face. For the first time since we first met, his physical presence intimidated me, and my muscles began to tighten, in spite of knowing full well that he could beat me to a pulp right here on this trail if he so desired. But Greg never touched me, and he eventually stepped away.

"Carrie just called me, freaking out about what happened in the coffee shop today. What the hell is the matter with you man?"

"She told you?" I gasped. "First of all, when did you become Carrie's shoulder to cry on? This is none of your business."

"Well she made it my business when she called me. So fuck you for saying that, and fuck you for putting me in this position by making me lie!"

"What position, Greg? Look, I'm sorry that she called you, but no one asked you to get in the middle of all of this."

"You put me in the middle of this the second we walked into that concert and you ran off with that girl. I didn't bust your balls about it, because I've been there, and we've all done stupid shit, and I figured you would have put this all behind you. But now I have your girlfriend crying to me on phone, asking me all these questions, like 'Did something happen in Portland?' and 'Did Jasper cheat on me?' What the fuck am I supposed to say to her Jass?" Greg had inched toward me again, his hands balled into fists.

"Look, nothing happened—"

"Stop. Just stop right there. Your infatuation with this girl has got to end. Right now. She was nothing, Jass. A pretty hipster. A one-night stand."

"Annabelle," I said, pausing for a few seconds. "Her name is Annabelle. And she was not just some pretty girl I met."

"Yeah? Well I don't give a shit what her name is. She's fogging your mind. A month ago, you would have never dreamed of putting Carrie through this, or talking about moving to New York. Where the hell did that come from, anyway?"

"It's a long story."

"All I know that is, if Carrie knew you were still taking to this girl—"

"But we're not, Greg," I interrupted. "That's the point! Annabelle and I haven't spoken since the concert. Hell, she might be dating some totally different guy by now. I have no idea Greg, and it's driving me absolutely crazy!"

My adrenaline was starting to fade, leaving my body so weak that I sat right down on the limestone path at Greg's feet. Finally, he sat down too, right next to me, and stared down the dark path, into the night.

"Look," I continued, "I know that Annabelle isn't the answer to my problems. I think she's just the one that brought them to light."

"And so that's it, then?" Greg asked, laughing

incredulously. "You spend one night with this girl and you're willing to throw your entire life away? Your job, your home. . . your future wife?"

"In other words, why would I throw away a sure thing?" Greg nodded.

"I'm not sure that's how I want to live, Greg. Should we be so petrified to take any chances just because there's something more stable already waiting for us?"

He still wouldn't look at me. I realized then that no matter how I tried to justify my actions, he would never agree with me. Figuring our conversation had reached its natural conclusion, I began to stand.

"Do you remember the night you met Carrie?" Greg asked.

I stopped, and looked down to see Greg's head hunched over, staring directly into the ground.

"Yes. Why?"

"That charity event," Greg went on, "that neither of us in a million years would ever have been caught dead attending. For the first time in my life, I was nervous about asking a girl out. I was completely outside of my comfort zone. And that's why you were there, Jass. To back me up. To give me courage. But you were distracted, weren't you?"

"I guess so, yeah."

"You became so immediately infatuated with Carrie," he continued, "that you were completely stuck in your bubble. And do you remember what happened with the person I was going after that night?"

"You told me it didn't work out."

"Right." Greg looked up at me and finally stood, holding my gaze. "Because she decided she wanted to date my roommate."

It was all I could do not to gasp out loud.

"You're the only person I know who has to do absolutely nothing other than stay the course you're on to get a life the rest of us would kill for." Greg finally looked away, back out into the night. "If you willingly choose to throw that all away, you're a bigger asshole than I thought."

Greg walked away, leaving me to stare after his dark receding outline. For a few moments, I tried to process his words, to disprove them in my mind. He had told me the girl's name at one point, hadn't he? She must have been a freshman or sophomore, a friend of a friend, one of the promiscuous cheerleaders or go-getter soccer players. Did he describe her features, her personality, her looks? Finally, I had to admit to myself that everything Greg had said must be true. Greg had had the hots for Carrie, and my interfering that night was the only thing that prevented their potential relationship from coming to fruition.

My stomach began to rumble, and I felt like vomiting. I had to leave that spot, which still felt so full of anger, frustration and disappointment. So I took off running. I sprinted back up the trail, through the woods, gasping in the night air.

At first I kept my arms close to my sides, assisting my run, but soon I let them burst free, flying open in a broad, unreciprocated hug, my figure now shaped like an eagle soaring up the path. I could have kept running for hours, for days, with no aim, just the sound of my breath and the burn of my legs. I didn't want the limestone path to end, and I could just run on and on, straight into the unknown world where there would be no betrayed girlfriend or disappointed best friend. But there was always an end, and when I finally reached it, I took only a moment's breath before I kept running: through the door to my apartment building, up the stairs, and straight to my bedroom, where I angrily kicked off my shoes and began screaming obscenities into my pillow. I punched my mattress and continued to scream until the cottony surface was soaked through with my tears and spit.

When my energy finally subsided, I leaned back against the wall behind my bed. Lingering tears blurred my vision, but I still could catch a glimpse of my opened email account on my laptop, which rested neatly on the center of my desk. And even from far away, the notification box was large enough that I could read it.

*How about Friday? —Ryan*

\*\*\*\*

Dear readers:

During a recent trip down memory lane, I re-read my first 'Jasper' post from a couple weeks ago, and ever since I've been plagued with sadness and regret. Not from the post itself—I'm still shocked by how much it resonated with my readers—but with how I chose to handle myself at the end of the concert. Simply put, I committed a grand mistake that I wish with every ounce of me I could take back.

When I first wrote about our night, I wrote that I wanted to end on a kiss, saying that the thought of our lips touching was more romantic than a steamy tryst followed by an awkward exit the next morning. Looking back, I still stand by what I said—the kiss was more romantic. But what I did wrong was place our fates in the hands of destiny, rather than within the realm of our own actions. There was no sense in doing the math: our chances of ever meeting again or recreating the magic of that night were extremely slim, so rather than face that low probability, I threw in the towel and left our destinies to fate. This was wrong. God it was wrong.

That night, before we parted, I took control of everything; it was me who led him to the forest, who serenaded him with poetic stories about an old rock, who tugged at his shirt and turned my lips toward his. I know now that Jasper was waiting for me to take control of our future, too. And though I had never connected with anyone the way I connected with him, I withheld my contact information on purpose—not because I was scared of commitment, but because I was scared this magical night would devolve into the same thing I've experienced so many times before. The explosive first interaction followed by the obligatory meet and greet. The tired talking points. The unintentional but inevitable fade-away. Our experience at Konacks was too special to risk turning into a mundane, forgettable relationship. So I did nothing.

But by choosing to do nothing, I was choosing to end everything. I was so concerned about making a tiny mistake that I inadvertently made a major one. And now, there's no way to go back. Despite the resources at our fingertips, unless Jasper arbitrarily decides to hop a plane back to Portland and wander the streets in the hopes that we happen to stumble upon one another, we will never see each other again. And that's fine. I get it, the law of averages and all. But knowing this is not the result of unforeseen circumstances but, rather, of my own actions pains me to the core.

Hoping for better days ahead.

Miss Mezzanine

5

Throughout the night, I kept repeating the words in Ryan's email aloud in my head and asking myself: *you don't think he meant* next *Friday, do you*? It was only Tuesday—just one full day after we had first met. Ryan couldn't possibly expect me to plan and execute an overnight trip to New York City in just forty eight hours, right? Then again, nothing about my entire interaction with Ryan thus far had seemed normal, so it would be foolish to rule anything out at this point. Still, analyzing every three-word email amounted to a scattered sleep, three hours at best.

When I realized that the day was beginning with or without me, I crawled out of bed and grabbed my cell phone. As expected, there were no calls or texts from Carrie, but there were two missed calls from my father. Unsure of what exactly he might want (other than that it would likely involve some form of scathing rebuke), I decided that the conversation would need to wait at least until after I ate something. I couldn't listen to his nonsense on an empty stomach.

Once I was dressed, I walked out into the living room.

Our analog clock on the wall read just after seven thirty. Greg's door was still shut. He hated waking up even a minute before absolutely necessary, but I still felt the urge to burst into his room and say sorry. Sorry for last night, sorry for putting him in such an awkward position during spring break, sorry for what happened nearly a year ago in front of the punch bowl. He might not accept my apologies, but at least there wouldn't be a growing tension between us. However, knowing that any apologies I made before 10 a.m. would likely make a night owl like Greg even more furious, I left alone.

Over the past few days Greg and I had gone through all of our breakfast food, so I decided to head over to The Dark Roast to grab a cup of coffee and a couple bagels. Hopefully that would hold me over until lunch. Shortly before I arrived, my phone vibrated in my pocket. I read my father's name on the caller ID. My instant reaction was to ignore him again, but that niggling possibility that he might be calling about something serious prompted me to flip the phone open.

"Dad? Is everything ok?" I asked.

"You know Jasper," he began, the irritation in his voice obvious from the very first word, "I might stop paying your cell phone bill if you refuse to answer my calls."

"I didn't refuse—" I began, but stopped, realizing that protesting was futile. "How are you doing? I'm on my way to grab breakfast before class."

"Yes, that seems to be the common theme. I called earlier to tell you that I spoke with Frank Harrison again briefly. Everything's all set for Friday morning. You can ride in to work with me; your interview begins promptly at nine."

"Uhh...," I began, but he continued without waiting for me to respond.

"Are you getting a ride home tomorrow night, or do you want me to come and pick you up?"

I stopped dead in my tracks, my empty stomach roiling. Despite the number of conversations we had had about this open position at my father's company, the fact that the interview was *this* Friday had entirely escaped me. And my dad's question couldn't have been more direct; avoiding or otherwise dodging a direct answer was impossible, no matter how skilled of an orator I might have been.

Say something. Just say something now.

"I'm not coming to the interview," I finally blurted out. The silence on the other end was so complete that I checked to make sure that my phone hadn't dropped the call. We were still connected. "Please tell Mr. Harrison I'm really sorry for having to cancel so last minute, but we'll just have to reschedule for another time."

"I'm extremely busy today Jasper, so I'm not going to waste any time going back and forth with you." If the technology existed, I'm sure my dad would have decked me directly through the phone. "You're coming home tomorrow and you are *not* cancelling. Frank switched around several meetings to accommodate this interview."

His formal work tone had disappeared, and every word now pulsed with anger. My knees began to weaken; I could either fold my hand or double down.

"I'm really sorry for having to cancel," I reiterated, "and if he can't reschedule another interview I fully understand. But I have something else going on that I can't rearrange."

"What?" he boomed. If he weren't already at his office, this would have evolved into a full-blown shouting match by now. "Classes? A test? You're graduating in two weeks Jasper—your teachers will understand if you have to move something around to establish your *future job*. And if they won't, tell me, and I'll call them myself."

"It's not a class or a test, dad."

"Then what is it?"

I knew my time was running out and that I'd either have to explain about New York City or make up something on the spot. Neither option seemed very appealing. So I instead, I tried the evasion tactic.

"Dad, my class is about to start. Can we talk about—"

"Don't even think about cutting me off Jasper Dietrich!" He was now actually yelling, the volume causing a rumbling echo in my phone. "I will not allow myself to be made a fool by my own son. Do you realize that cancelling on Frank completely destroys your chances of getting this job? I'm not going to beg him to give you another chance."

"Well maybe that's what I want!"

I flipped the phone shut immediately before my father had a chance to respond. And then, knowing that he'd likely call me back in a fiery rage, I shut the phone off altogether and stuck it back in my pocket. I recalled several experiences throughout my life when I had pissed off my father—talking back to my mother, earning less than a 3.5 grade point average, getting caught drinking at a party—but never once had I walked away, stormed out or hung up. I could picture my father breathing heavily at his office, walking back and forth behind his enormous mahogany desk, trying to form a coherent sentence as he spewed jumbled, angry words at my voicemail. But for me, once I hung up the phone, an instant euphoria took over. I had never felt better.

I walked into McLaren Hall. I tried my best to pay attention to my Gothic Literature class, which was difficult given my teacher's screechy nails-on-a-chalkboard voice. Within a few minutes, any attempts were abandoned, as I began thinking about the logistics of getting to New York. I hadn't actually told anybody I was going, or even confirmed the meeting with Ryan, but the second I hung up on my father, I knew that I had officially made my decision.

However, this was easier said than done: for starters, how was I going to get there, and once I arrived, where was I going to stay? I had used up every penny from my summer job to go to Portland over spring break, and the money my parents deposited into my account at the beginning of each semester was at an all-time low. A trip like this would cost hundreds of dollars, which meant I'd be dumping almost everything I had left into this New York City voyage. And after this morning's discussion with my father, I'd rather someone throw me to a pack of wolves than ask my parents for any financial help.

When our professor had finally exhausted her mind-numbing discussion on Mary Shelley, I quickly exited down the hallway to the computer lab in the library. There was already an email in my inbox from Ryan with no subject line. A lump suddenly formed in my throat. This was it. I had delayed too long, and now I had lost my chance. This was a New York City man—he moved fast and wanted his workers to move fast, too. His email was probably terse and polite and said something along the lines of "Thanks for your interest, but in the twelve hours during which you pissed and moaned, we filled every position at Rydel Media." With the lump growing fast in my throat, I clicked on the email.

*You should probably read this.* –Ryan

There were a series of documents attached, all about Rydel Media, which I guess meant I hadn't blown it just yet. I felt relieved. The lump vanished, and I could breathe normally again. At that point, I didn't hesitate: I wrote him back and told him Friday was perfect, that I was coming, and to please confirm the time and place. Minutes later, he responded with all the details.

I browsed through the attachments quickly. Most were just marketing materials about the company, glossy brochures filled with fluffy text and colorful graphics highlighting how great and innovative Rydel Media was. But I noticed some of the things he sent me included scanned handwritten notes, too, some which were even personally addressed to me. Ryan wasn't just sending me materials to brush up on my knowledge of his company and the industry; he was guiding me toward a successful interview.

Thus, I officially began my two-day cram session, skipping the rest of my classes and replacing any knowledge of business ethics or gothic literature with new advertising and marketing concepts. I imagined Ryan thought I already knew about most of the terms and topics he was sending me, and that if anything, the information would just serve as a refresher. In actuality, though I earned solid grades, I didn't retain a lot of the information from my other classes that I would likely need to ace an interview. Therefore, not only did I need to brush up on what I had already supposedly learned as a business major, I also needed to memorize all of this industry-specific information and then act as if I knew more than I really did.

My only break consisted of arranging the logistics of my trip: browsing online through all of New York City's hotel offerings, trying my best to find something even slightly affordable. After all, I only had a few hundred bucks to blow on this trip. When I finally caved and booked one about a mile from Rydel Media, the next step up was booking my flight. Then I saw how much even an eight-hour flight with three layovers cost, so I abandoned that route. Train? Not much better. Thankfully a bus route from Pittsburgh to New York picked up passengers at a station not too far from here, and it wouldn't break the bank. I laughed when I booked my trip, realizing that at twenty-two years old, this would be the first time I had ever travelled alone. Alone and broke.

With my butt now numb and my hunger resurfacing, I decided to take a break and head to the cafeteria. I hadn't realized that while arguing with my father, I had actually skipped breakfast. I printed out the rest of Ryan's materials and grabbed my phone, hesitating for several seconds before pressing the 'send' button and turning it on.

Normally, when I received a voicemail, my phone would vibrate for five seconds. I imagined that in mere moments, my phone would be shaking so much that it would enter seizure mode and start foaming at the mouth. I stood still, waiting to see how many times Carrie, my father, and Greg had called or texted me. But nothing happened. Not a single call. Not a single text. Just saved battery power.

The typical grease-filled smell of the cafeteria was easier to ignore this time, since my hunger overrode any typical displeasure I had with the food. But I couldn't tune out the endless conversations and infinite chatter of my underclassmen behind me in line, ranging from girls complaining about immature boys, to boys fawning over hot girls. Sophomore stuff. I could only smile, knowing their priorities would be shifting so much in just a year or two. I grabbed a seat in the corner, quickly ate my pasta and marinara, and then continued to do what I had been doing all day: reading.

A little later, I hopped in line for seconds and checked to see if anyone reached out to me yet. Still nothing. If anything, the lack of communication served as a reality check on my ego. Plus, it convinced me that I hadn't given Carrie enough credit. She was nothing if not determined, and even our arguments couldn't detract her from completing whatever homework assignment or campus event rested on her agenda.

Still my decision had been made, my trip was booked, and simply ignoring Carrie for another day meant both of us walking into our interviews with this massive uncertainly hanging over our heads. Plus the onus was now on me in terms of reinstating the lines of communication. At this point, she had been dragged along on this ride blindfolded for long enough. So I folded up the materials, stuck them and my phone in my jeans pocket and headed in the direction of her dorm, not knowing exactly what I needed to do or what I was going to say.

Hours had passed and by now it was seven thirty. Wednesdays usually constituted one of Carrie's designated study nights, so I knew she'd be in her dorm with her face planted in a book. I chose to show up without any invitation, fearing that calling her or otherwise giving any advanced notice would prompt her to tell me to fuck off and ruin my resolve. Still, my dread of this confrontation severely slowed my pace. Every time my foot hit the pavement, I second-guessed myself and considered turning around. When I finally arrived, I tapped the door lightly, maybe subconsciously hoping Carrie wouldn't answer.

She didn't. But Stacey did.

She flashed me a look of sass and disapproval; I guess Carrie had shared with her all of the details of our earlier confrontation. Any temporary likeability toward me from yesterday had long since disappeared; she was back in Stacey mode.

"Is Carrie here?" I asked. I kept my expression as impassive as possible.

"Carrie doesn't want to see you, Jass."

"So that's a yes?" I stood there, watching her judge me. Ironically, having her stare at me like I had somehow abused Carrie made me want to punch this girl in the face. Eventually, she stepped aside and let me in, watching my every move as though I might be concealing a firearm or other large weapon. We entered the living room alone; I made a beeline directly for Carrie's room to avoid any extra bit of interaction with Stacey.

"CARRIE, JASS IS HERE!" she screamed, as if Carrie needed to be warned just to allow more time to whip out her can of mace. Carrie's bedroom door was ajar, so I walked in. As expected, Carrie was sprawled out on her bed reading a Psychology book. She stared up at me without setting the book down. Her silence was deafening. But I knew that look: pissed.

I closed the door behind me and pulled a seat up next to

her bed. Her lack of silence or movement indicated that she was waiting for me to make the first move, but I was completely at a loss. Despite my best attempts to craft some sort of explanatory monologue during my walk over, I chose instead to wing it. But now seeing her face-to-face and knowing that I needed to say something—anything—to try and rectify the situation, I had no idea how to form any words.

"Hi," was all I muttered.

"Hi."

"Studying for an exam?"

"For my interview, actually," she replied. She flashed me the cover of her book, *The Psychology of Interaction*. "According to this book, interviews are tied to the same basic tenets as modern psychological theory. Just a different subset."

I chose to not look at the book, since that would likely provoke a follow-up question about her interview, and instead get to the point. I could feel her bedroom walls closing in on me. My throat burned as I struggled to speak.

"Do you remember our first date?" I finally blurted out.

"Yes. What about it?" She finally set her book down.

I stood up. The numbness from earlier was starting to recur, and my legs were cramping. For a second, I felt like a teacher standing in front of his classroom. I tried to ignore the height difference between my standing and her lying on the bed as I continued.

"You were so assertive, so confident in everything that you did, like it was less of a date and more of an assignment you wanted to ace." She turned to me, insulted, but I put my hand up and laughed. "That's not a criticism Carrie. You kept me on my toes, forced me to up my game. And that never changed, not once in the last ten months that we've dated. You always have a handle on everything, and it was what I admired about you the most. But now it scares me."

"Why, Jass? What changed?"

"Me." Suddenly, somehow, I was sitting next to her on the bed. I felt much more relaxed. "For the first time in my life, Carrie, I feel like it's ok to stray away from what's been expected of me. That if I want to settle in Pittsburgh and get a shitty job at my father's company, I can, but if I don't, there are other options. Paths that don't include. . . ."

"Me?"

"Yes, you."

Carrie's face scrunched up, her lips pursuing and her eyes shutting. Seconds later, I saw the first tear drip from her left eye. I couldn't help but stare at first; I had never seen her cry. Then I wanted nothing but to turn away. It was heartbreaking.

"Look," I finally went on, "you and Greg have it all figured out. You know where A is, you know where B is, and you know exactly how you're getting from one to the other. But that's not me. It just took a few days away from everything to realize that I am allowed to admit that."

"So something *did* happen in Portland?"

I thought about Greg yelling at me last night, and how his anger was less about me and more about wanting to protect Carrie. Even if he wasn't my best friend, I imagined that he still could have revealed everything about my trip if he saw any benefit. But I also imagined that, like me, Greg probably felt that she was already in so much pain from what was already happening with our relationship that telling her about Annabelle and the concert had little to offer but even more pain.

Carrie interrupted my thoughts. "Stop being a fucking coward and tell me the truth!"

My throat was on fire. I knew what the truth meant: flirting, kissing Annabelle, touching her in a way I had never touched Carrie, pining for her, all of the things I had spewed to Greg on the trail last night. Carrie was so close to wrestling all of it out of me. And though I knew the words would set both of us free—me of the burden of lying and hiding something so damaging, her of all the suspicions and second-guessing—I still couldn't bring myself to utter the truth.

"Nothing happened, Carrie."

The lie was an act of cowardice shielded in decency; still, it was the only way to protect her. If I told her everything, the full betrayal of my actions, it would likely instill trust issues that would be difficult to recover from. I didn't want Carrie to have to worry about the next guy that came along, the *right* one, perhaps.

For a moment we remained still, sitting side-by-side on her bed, Carrie still wiping tears from her face. She studied me intensely, and I didn't blink or move even the smallest muscle. It was a test I normally would have failed; Carrie was, after all, a Psychology minor. However, this time I had more on the line than ever before, and eventually she turned away, finally believing me. At least I hoped so.

"You were supposed to be there, every step," she said. She continued to cry.

"I can be," I responded, "but I'm freeing you, Carrie. I'm freeing you from having to worry about us when you should be focusing on the things that are most important to you. You're going to nail your interview Friday, and it'll be just the beginning of a life full of great things. I don't want to be a distraction."

"And what about New York?"

"Who knows," I said. I considered leaving out the more definite details, but she was going to find out, one way or another. "We'll see what happens when I go there tomorrow for my interview."

She flinched for a moment, then nodded her head a few times, in acceptance.

"I'm sure you're going to knock it out of the park, Jass," she said. "You could talk your way out of a death sentence." She stood up and walked to her door, opening it and then standing still. "You should probably get back to your apartment; looks like we both have a ton of work to do."

I hesitated, watching her try to hold back any further tears, unsuccessfully. I wanted to apologize more—say that I was sorry, since I realized that word had never actually come out of my mouth—but I knew dragging things out would just make it all worse. With a heavy heart, I forced myself to leave. We had both delivered the messages that needed to be delivered. The rest would come with patience and time apart.

When I walked back into the living room, Stacey was nowhere to be found. I closed the front door behind me, knowing that my relationship with Carrie was over, even though neither of us had actually said the words. And as much as I wanted to fix Carrie's sadness, I wished even more that Stacey would have been around when I left. If there was ever a time I deserved to be shredded by the gauntlet, it was now.

****

Dear readers,

I'm often so busy singing the praises of the more talented writers and performers out there that I sometimes forget to remind myself of a basic fact: I am an artist. Am I a great artist? No, but I certainly love to learn, and I think it's fair to say that my output has improved over time (in both my blog writing and everything outside of it). So perhaps it's time to rant about why I'm actually here, and what the Earth has shown me about both the mysteries and joys of artistic creation.

I don't subscribe to any established religion, as so many of these institutionalized groups tend to be corrupted by those in power and lean more toward fear-mongering than enlightenment. Still, I need to look no further than the ocean waves that lightly sweep across the coast or the heaven-reaching California Redwoods to know that something out there created this beautiful globe of existence. And while scientific theories and mathematical calculations can provide the explanation for such beauty, I believe that God places artists on this Earth to create sights and sounds that allow us to experience the world in its purest form. In other words, artists are the megaphones and magnifying glasses for Earth's splendor. In a sense, we're all creators (or at least have the ability to be), and so I pride myself in sharing that common bond with so much talent, which is what I think drew me here in the first place.

The name *Miss Mezzanine* was derived from my basic view of the world when I had just graduated college, and the balance between landing a cushy job and remaining true to myself was called into question. Prior to this point, my writings were kept locked up in a personal journal, my drawings stayed hidden behind my bedroom furniture, my songs confined within the walls of my dormitory. My mind rested in a mezzanine between my future career and my passions, as either I needed to hop on that train of uncertainty and focus on actually doing something with my art, or accept the reality and focus solely on the nine to fives in the world ahead of me. So starting this blog helped serve as my transition from one to the other, offering a way for me to sustain my love for art while also recognizing that my life was entering a new phase.

What better way to find myself and my role in this artistic world than to learn, study, and write about the other artists who surround me? And while many things have changed since, I still remain in that mezzanine, continuing to pursue my love of art while also recognizing the necessity of holding down a job that enables me to feed and cloth myself. Sometimes you have to compromise in life, but that doesn't mean you have to sell out.

It's funny—despite the importance that each concert, each album, each film plays in my life today, I still hid this blog (and everything else I do) from Jasper. Why? Initially I tried to justify this decision to myself by claiming that I wanted to shield my blog's anonymity. The truth is, though, that at the time, I didn't want my writing to shape his perception of me. Certain artists (hopefully NOT me) carry a pretentious attitude, and so pigeonholing myself as An Artist might have shifted his belief in who I am. Does that make sense? Probably not. But I see now that it was a mistake to hide something that constitutes such a major part of myself.

And then I have to wonder what *he* chose to hold back. What if he's out there in Pittsburgh writing the next Great Gatsby, or performing Debussy in a grand concert hall, or painting the next Mona Lisa at some off-campus studio apartment? So many questions, and I so crave those answers, just to learn how close (or far apart) our philosophies are of how we see the world and our proper places within it.

I am an artist. And I'm sorry I never told him that. But I'm telling you, dear readers, loud and clear. And maybe, someday, I'll have a second chance to tell him, too.

Still here,

Miss Mezzanine

6

"Rise and shine sleepy head."

Greg's eyes flickered a bit, still encased in a crusty coating from just a few hours of sleep. He didn't respond well to wake-up calls, so his body was often in motion before his mind could catch up. He managed to stretch a bit and even stare me dead in the eyes once or twice before he actually recognized who was hovering over him.

"What the hell man? It's seven o'clock," he moaned, each word representing about half of a coherent syllable. I didn't respond, just continued to hold my creepy smile, hoping that my over-the-top 'sadistic uncle' approach would lighten the mood a bit. Despite his recent anger toward me, Greg was still a sucker for a good tease, and pulling him out of his slumber in this maniacal way was my best attempt to break the ice. He eventually couldn't ignore me any longer, my heavy, overly loud and slow breaths interfering with his likely attempts to try and go back to sleep, so he finally sat up.

"What?"

I stood up, revealing to Greg the pair of mesh shorts I

wore and the soccer ball in my hands. I spun the ball in the air and released, aiming it at his chest. Out of pure instinct, he caught it, preventing it from falling on the ground. He launched it back at me. Even while lying down, his delivery still knocked my breath out when it made impact.

"I know about Carrie," he said.

Carrie had likely called Greg the moment I left, either to beg him to talk some sense into me or to lament about how much of an asshole I was. The latter option was far more likely, so I chose not to pry for additional details.

"Get dressed, grab your soccer shoes, and let's hit the field. Come on."

"Jass it's—"

I walked out, slamming the door shut before he had a chance to finish.

Our two-story apartment complex formed a square around a central courtyard, which was about half the size of a football field. Usually the courtyard served as the primary location for pickup soccer games, where even the freshmen and sophomores gathered to play against some of the more athletic juniors and seniors. I rarely partook, but Greg was among the best of those who hadn't actually made the school's soccer team. Given how early it was, the field was empty, and I felt like a gladiator in the Coliseum on the bare grass.

I stood there, wondering if Greg would leave me hanging or finally make the trek outside. If he did come out, that would mean he might be open to some sort of an apology, which would be a relief, because going on my journey hundreds of miles east with my best friend still mad at me would be terrible.

"Hey asshole!" a voice shouted, and before I could even turn around, the soccer ball hit me square in the back. I looked up to see Greg on our balcony, arms crossed.

"Oh I'm sorry," I responded, throwing the ball back up to the second floor, "I didn't realize the Powder Puff season started so early. Maybe you need a running start to throw the ball a little harder?"

Greg turned away, taking his time to walk down the steps. About thirty seconds later, he was standing in front of me, tossing the ball up in the air and catching it. He didn't have a readable expression on his face but I knew Greg: he wanted to smile.

"You dragged me out of bed, and now we're standing here. What's next, kiss and make up?"

"Not quite." I ran to the other end of the courtyard, encouraging him to kick the ball to me. While I sprinted, Greg brought his leg back and back down, kicking the ball as hard as he could. The sun shined down on me, causing a blur in the little speck of black patches spinning through the air. I planted my feet firmly on the ground, blocking the sun with my left hand, and managing to catch the ball with my right.

"Touchdown!" I screamed, spiking the ball.

"Wrong game, moron. Plus, your ass would have been tackled at the forty yard line before you even made the catch," he responded. He walked toward me as he spoke, and I met him halfway between his kick and my catch.

We were back at square one, but his simple act of kicking a soccer ball proved that he was at least willing to engage. At the moment, that's all I needed. Even though he still looked angry.

"You fucked up Jass—" he began.

"I know," I interrupted.

"Carrie's not going to wait—"

"I don't expect her to," I interrupted again. "But that's not why we're here." I hadn't stopped thinking about Carrie—images of her mascara running down her face still flashed through my mind—but what was done was done. I tried not to let the memories of her tears distract me.

"Four years of friendship," I went on. "All the shit that we've been through. For Christ's sake, living together.

We've always able to shrug off the bad stuff. This needs to be the same, Greg. I lost Carrie last night—"

"By choice."

"Yes, by choice!" I yelled, trying to contain my frustration. "But I can't lose my best friend, too." Silence. It was impossible to tell what he was thinking, so I barreled on. "I swear I didn't know you were interested in Carrie, Greg. I never in a million years would have chased after her if I had."

"I know you didn't, Jass," he said. He sat down on the grass in front of me. "And I know you never wanted to hurt her either. You're not an asshole, and I tried my best to tell her that last night. But goddamn if you don't make stupid decisions sometimes."

"You don't und—" I tried to say, but he cut me off.

"And when you utter that bullshit about me not understanding, you make me want to rip your fucking arms off. Despite what you believe—that you have some amazing insight into the future that nobody else does— you're beyond wrong. I warned you not to go down this path."

"Coming from a guy who decided to go to school like five thousand miles away from his family for no other reason than wanting to get away? You knew nothing about Tundra, about Pittsburgh, whether you'd hate it, love it, tolerate it. You took a chance on this place, and now look. You couldn't imagine being anywhere else."

"This is different."

"Why?"

"Because, man, I didn't have someone like Carrie back in Portland. You do!"

I nodded, knowing he didn't realize that his comment sparked a thought of Annabelle, and not Carrie. Still, I realized that trying to convince Greg of anything at this point was futile.

"How about I let you punch me once in the face and we

call it even?" I joked. He started to laugh but caught himself.

"Don't tempt me Jass!" I could see his smiling muscles twitch. I helped him back up.

"Come on, one good one. You said yourself you wanted to. But not too hard; I need to look good tomorrow. Don't want these people thinking I'm part of some underground fight club."

He finally laughed, pulling his fist back as if he actually might do it. I shut my eyes, playing along, knowing full well he wouldn't. Instead, he lightly punched me in the stomach. More of a love tap, really. In slow motion, I pretended as if he had knocked the wind out of me, falling to the ground with over-the-top theatrics.

"There's nothing else I can do to stop you, huh?" He reached out his hand to help me up.

"No," I responded, taking it, "but there is something you can to do help me get there."

"What?"

"Give me a ride to the bus station?"

About thirty minutes later, I was in the passenger seat of Greg's Camry, my tiny roller suitcase stuffed with two days' worth of essentials. We drove to the station in amicable silence, arriving about fifteen minutes prior to the scheduled departure. There was no sign of the bus yet, but about a dozen other people were lined up along the curb, leaning against a concrete wall or sitting on their carry-on luggage. Greg pulled over to the side of the road and turned on his blinkers.

"Did you pack an extra pair of underwear? Socks in case it's cold? Emergency contacts?" I punched Greg in the shoulder and he laughed. He put the car in park.

"Listen Jass," he said, growing serious, "this guy is the gatekeeper to an entirely new future. So be friendly, but be humble."

"I'm not stupid, Greg."

"That remains to be seen. But since you've stepped up to the Roulette table, taken your whole bankroll and bet it on this one guy, I guess I'd just say: keep your eye on that wheel."

He wished me good luck one more time as I pulled my suitcase out of the back. Then he beeped once and was gone. In that moment, as I watched the back of Greg's silver Camry fade away into the distance, I realized this trip was actually happening. Just a few short days ago, I was sitting in a dive bar near campus, joking around with a former alumnus about his views on life, and now here I was, en route to the Big Apple.

Minutes later, the bus arrived. I jumped on and snatched a seat in the very back row. The bus smelled a bit funny, and an older gentleman sitting in the seat next to me had already passed out. With nothing else to do, I popped on my music player, which proved to be a mild sedative. With my weariness from the past three days finally kicking in, I finally dozed off, just like my drooling neighbor next to me.

"Buddy?" I was pulled back to consciousness by my elderly bus neighbor shaking my arm. I could feel that the ordinary vibrations of the bus were missing; we weren't moving. The moist feeling on my face prompted me to wipe off a stream of drool that was now running down my chin.

It took me a while to fully come back to life, since I didn't want to let go of the dream I had just had. It was the first time I'd ever dreamt of my time with Annabelle: a combination of erotic fantasies blended with real memories from the concert. In reality, my mental visions of her were slipping away, her facial characteristics blurring together into one vague image, like a police sketch from a lapsed memory. But in the dream everything was so clear, and all of her physical features and expressions that I remembered so fondly from that night bright and vivid.

We were stopped at a busy intersection, and without even looking out the window, I could just *feel* that I was in New York City. Maybe it was the air, or the noise, both more noticeable and potent than when I had departed from Tundra. I waited patiently as everyone else exited the bus. Eventually it was my turn, and I walked forward, the last person off the double decker. I took a long, deep breath, looked around and immediately admired everything I was seeing.

There were four skyscrapers within a hundred yards of me, all at least fifty stories high. People zoomed past me speaking at least three different languages. A man stood at a food cart, joyously handing out chicken on a stick to a teenager and his mom. Steam poured out of a sewer grate at my feet, the heat nearly blasting me in the face. Trash overflowed. Horns honked every second. The entire city of Pittsburgh could fit on this one street.

The street was overfilled with yellow taxi cabs whizzing by. I grabbed my small suitcase from the luggage compartment and walked to the corner. I had never hailed a cab before, so I took my cue from what I had seen in movies and held out a hand. At least two dozen cabs ignored me before one finally stopped. I threw my suitcase in the trunk and hopped in, scrounging around my pockets to find the address of the hotel I had booked.

"Umm . . . four two five east sixty-first street," I said. He waved to me from the front seat and pulled out into traffic.

The ride took about fifteen minutes. As we drove, I just sat there, watching the aggressive cab driver weave in and out of traffic as if he were playing a video game, completely heedless of the thousands of other drivers and pedestrians in his path. I felt sure we would crash into one—or several—other vehicles at any moment, if we didn't run over someone and their dog first. And though all the other drivers also seemed to disregard every driving rule I had ever learned, the pedestrians were even worse. The 'walk' and 'don't walk' signs seemed to be nothing more than loose guidelines. Groups would surge out into oncoming traffic, only hurrying slightly if they were at risk of getting smacked head-on by one of the cabs on the road. Their self-confidence was astounding. Clearly, these people belonged to New York City just as much as it belonged to them. No city demonstrated that level of synergy.

When we reached the hotel, I jumped out of the cab.

"No pay!" the driver screamed.

"I'm sorry," I muttered, mortified. "How much?"

I couldn't decipher exactly what the cab driver said in reply, so I tossed him a twenty-dollar bill and he seemed to be happy. The cab driver took off, yelling in some foreign language before I could even utter the words 'thank you'.

I now stood in front of an enormous Hilton knockoff, a building so tall and yet still so cheap that a part of me feared what waited for me inside. Still, one night in this hotel was over two hundred dollars, which was a good chunk of change given how little time I'd be spending in my room.

I checked in and was told that my room was on the seventh floor, which for some reason gave me the illusion that I had professional credibility. Entering the room further enforced that illusion. I had only stayed in a handful of hotels in my life, but this one was by far the fanciest. The TV was larger than any I've ever owned, the shower looked like it belonged in the future with its fifteen water pressure settings, and there was even a candy dish near the bed. Free candy!

The clock read nearly six, and the daylight would be disappearing soon. This didn't bother me; I had seen New York City at night in so many movies that I couldn't picture experiencing the city any other way. I hadn't packed a map, nor did I possess any general sense of the city's geography apart from its grid-like structure, but I wanted to trek to

Times Square to see if it was actually as entertaining and poetic as I've been led to believe. Or maybe Madison Park. Or Central Park. Or any number of other hot spots that I had observed over years and years of watching movies.

In his last email to me, Ryan had given me his phone number and suggested calling when I arrived at the hotel. I couldn't quite determine whether he actually wanted to hang out the night before the interview or if this was nothing more than a nice gesture.

I sat on the corner of my bed, agonizing over whether or not to try and contact him. My first and most important interview was only fifteen hours away; speaking with Ryan in person again could either benefit me greatly or prove to be a fatal mistake. In the end I decided to compromise: I'd just shoot him one quick text to let him know I had made it—that way, if he didn't want to respond, it would be easier to ignore my text than an actual phone call. Minutes later, however, he texted back:

*Few of us from office hanging at apt in Upper East Side. You should stop by. Here's address...*

I re-read Ryan's text a dozen times, agonizing over my next move. Finally, I decided that his use of the word 'should' rather than something like 'can' or 'may' meant that this was a good idea, a pre-interview to my actual time in the hot seat.

I glanced at myself one more time in the mirror, making sure my appearance could at least pass as presentable, then shut the door behind me. Before I left the hotel, I took a detour to the bar, ordering a rum and ginger ale to try and calm my nerves. One sip turned into three large chugs, and before I knew it, I had called the bartender back over to order a second drink. I pulled the address out of my pocket.

"Can I walk here?" I asked.

"It'll take you maybe thirty minutes," he responded,

topping off my drink, "or a ten minute cab ride, fifteen if you hop on the E train."

I tried my best to maintain a look of confidence, but he saw right through me. He searched through a scattered drawer and pulled out a map. He then proceeded to draw out my entire route in red ink. I thanked him profusely, tipping him generously and chugging the rest of my drink in one big gulp before I took off.

With every intersection I reached, I tried to wait at least a minute before I crossed the street, still recalling that frightening cab ride. I also managed to peek my head in at least a dozen different stores on each block, amazed at how many businesses existed in such a concentrated area. I was aware that my awestruck gaze probably pegged me as an obvious tourist, so I tried walking faster, even jaywalking a couple of times, just to try and fit in with the rest of the locals. After all, I didn't want to get pickpocketed. By the time I got there, I realized that the thirty-minute walk had felt like fifteen. Had I taken the E train after all?

I arrived a few minutes before seven o'clock. I double-checked the address to make sure I was at the right spot—I was. The apartment was bright blue brick sandwiched between two much smaller apartments, and its quaint, classic construction made it look like it belonged in Charleston, South Carolina rather than New York City. I looked down at my semi-wrinkled khakis and a button-down shirt, second-guessing my choice of attire. "I look like fucking Wally Cleaver," I muttered to myself. For a second I thought of turning around and buying an "I heart NY" shirt from the vendor up the street, just to look less foolish. That, though, would probably have been even worse.

"Jass!" Ryan Felton had just opened the front door. It was too late to back out now. "Come on in!"

Inside, an immediate wave of mainstream rap music pounded my eardrums. I recognized the artists, none of which I particularly admired. Past the main entrance, we walked into a small living room where five people were sitting on the two couches, facing each other and playing some type of card game. I could make out ten or so other people mingling in a nearby dining room and kitchen. Ryan put his arm around my shoulder and blinked the lights, quieting the room.

"Hey everybody, this is Jass. He's up here for the night from Tundra, my alma mater. He has a big job interview tomorrow at Rydel!" The crowd starting making ohh and ahh sounds. "So let's give him some love and respect and try not to scare him away before he even steps foot in the building!"

Ryan offered me a drink, and I told him that a beer would do. The rum and ginger ales from earlier still swished around my stomach, and while I wouldn't say I was that buzzed, I was far enough along that anything stronger than a beer might have pushed me into that realm. He stepped away, forcing me to interact with other people if I didn't want to stand there awkwardly by myself.

I approached the couch and took the one remaining empty seat. For a moment, all I did was observe; the five of them were playing some sort of vulgar guessing game. I kept my mouth shut, because I had suddenly developed this paranoid idea that one of them was a mole who would report my inappropriate behavior to the Rydel interviewers tomorrow, and I'd be sent packing before I even got to pull out my resume. Eventually, though, one girl on the couch leaned over to me.

"Interview tomorrow, huh? I remember mine like it was yesterday." She stuck out her hand, and I shook it. "I'm Theresa."

"Jass. Any good tips?" I tried not to stare, but her two tattoos jumped out at me. One was a tiny yellow sunflower on her left wrist, and the other was a spider web on her side, only partially exposed by her shirt, which had ridden up slightly. Apart from that, she looked fairly run-of-the mill, comparable to most of the other girls at the party: blonde hair, blue eyes. Girls like that apparently were predisposed to working in Advertising.

"Well for one, hide any inhibitions you may be feeling. Don't wear your nerves on your sleeve. Oh, and flash more of that cute smile."

I blushed, but before I could comment, Ryan rejoined a couple seconds later and tossed me a beer. It was so cold I almost dropped it on the floor. Once I had control, I twisted it open and took a big swig.

"What's the play this round?" Ryan asked. He placed himself on the arm of the one couch, leaning over the side and almost falling on top of one of the girls. Based on this and his general interactions with the people in the room, I gathered that he led this group of people, and they followed with ease. Much like his behavior and general attitude at Tundra, he quickly took command of his surroundings, and even when he asked a simple question, the game stopped dead in its tracks as they all rushed to answer him.

Theresa pulled out a small card and read, "The buzzword is 'cock'."

"Ok, freshman," Ryan said, pointing to me. A lump formed in my throat. All eyes were suddenly on me. "You might as well hit the ground running if you want to make it in the glorious world of advertising. So you heard the buzzword. Now the purpose of the game is to say a famous movie quote, but switching out one of the nouns in the quote with the buzzword. People are supposed to write stuff down and use scoring cards or whatever, but we just play on the fly. So go."

I sat there. Everyone stared.

"Me?" I asked, stalling for time. Ryan nodded. Was this for real? I had arrived at this stranger's apartment (I still wasn't sure who the owner was), and now a group of five people were sitting around, waiting for me to insert the word 'cock' into a pop culture reference. Thankfully, my mind stored an encyclopedia of random movie quotes, and so it was just a matter of picking the right one to apply to this situation.

"Cock, for lack of a better word, is good," I said. Like a defense mechanism, I took to the beer, drinking nearly half of it while the rest of them sat in silence. Theresa shrugged her shoulders first but then only stared, as if seductively waiting for me to move so she could pounce like a lioness. Ryan didn't even flinch, not moving until he took another sip of his drink. He slapped his leg.

"This kid's got balls, I'll give him that." Ryan lowered himself onto the couch, slouching into the corner. "Uses a quote that pertains to the very location that he's trying to break into tomorrow. Very good, Jass."

"Oh yeah! Greed!" Theresa exclaimed, rejoining the conversation. She turned to Ryan. "But wait, we work on Madison Avenue?"

Ryan silenced her with one hand. "So is it, Jass?"

"Is what, what?" I asked.

"Is greed good?"

"I dunno," I replied. "I mean, I guess we're all greedy sometimes, right?"

"You have to be prepared to talk about these things, Jass," he said. It was the first time Ryan looked bothered, annoyed even. "There are no shades of grey in this world, only black and white. Someone asks you a question at work, you can't bumble through your answers; you must know the facts. Anticipate every unknown. Are you prepared to do that?"

The music, still blaring in the other room, felt like it was on mute. My heart started to pound so hard that it dictated my breaths, which had doubled in pace during the last five seconds. I could feel imaginary hives starting to form on my chest. Everyone was watching me, and I knew that saying something stupid would leave a first impression I'd likely never shake.

114

"I am prepared, Ryan, and if you'd like, I'm more than happy to teach you, as well."

The couch crowd erupted in laughter, like Ryan and I had been in the midst of an insult battle, and I had struck the final blow. Ryan didn't move but rather twitched, eventually letting his guard down and smiling again. He stood, walked over to the other side of the couch where I sat, and put his arm around my shoulder.

"You see? You see? Didn't I tell you this kid was smart?" he exclaimed. I could breathe again, relieved beyond belief that my sarcastic response was taken for what it was: complete hyperbole. He continued:

"Most people can't fire back like that, Jass. Even at a party like this, people under pressure just curl up and freeze. But you didn't, you doubled down and stood firm. That's what you have to do to survive here. Because the fact of the matter is that no one gives a shit about you except yourself. So when someone pushes you, you push back, but ten times harder. Nice job, kid."

Ryan put his fingers to his lips, insinuating smoking a cigarette, and motioned to Theresa. She stood up, and that's when I noticed Ryan motioning to me, too. I snuck off the couch and followed both of them. We cut through the dining room to the back door, where Ryan fetched another beer and tossed it to me, even though I hadn't finished drinking my first.

Outside, we emerged onto a small stoop that sat beneath a fire escape. The temperature had dropped a few degrees since my walk over, and I shivered lightly under my lightweight clothing. Theresa dug through her pockets and pulled out a joint. She handed it to Ryan, who immediately lit it and took a puff. An instant flashback of me choking on smoke inside Greg's car on our way to Konacks ran through my mind.

"Want a hit?" Ryan asked. I shook my head and laughed out loud. I hadn't smoked since Konacks, but a good part of me believed that Ryan wanted to insert me into a potentially uncomfortable situation to see how I responded. So the only thing to do was play it cool.

"You guys sure do party a lot here for a Thursday," I said. "I thought that sort of stuff ended in college."

"Well, this isn't your typical Thursday," Ryan shot back. "We're sort of celebrating. The year treated our company well, so our company treated us well today."

"Bonuses," Theresa chimed in as she took the joint from Ryan and took her first hit. She coughed lightly and passed it back.

"But that doesn't matter to you," Ryan went on. "What matters is that the powers that be are also in a good mood. And when that's the case, it's a good time for Tonberry to be interviewing you for a new job. So consider yourself lucky."

"Tonberry?" I asked.

"Stanley Tonberry, our supervisor," Theresa replied. "Hard as nails, very flat, no sense of humor whatsoever."

"Basically a huge jerkoff," Ryan laughed. "Well, not really. But he'll definitely come across that way tomorrow. He will also ask tough questions and demand specific answers. So be prepared to think on your feet."

I thought about all of the material that Ryan had sent me over the past couple of days but didn't want to mention it in front of Theresa. Ryan looked at her and then motioned to me. "So Theresa, I believe that Jass and his girlfriend just broke up, no?"

What? I definitely hadn't told him about Carrie; it certainly wasn't something I would have written to him in a random email, and we hadn't spoken since the dive bar. I laughed, afraid to confirm, deny, or otherwise divulge any other information. Carrie had been through enough these past few weeks that the least she deserved was not to be gossiped about by a stranger at a party hundreds of miles away. Ryan may have sensed my reservations, but it didn't matter; a crowd of girls poured outside, pulling Theresa back inside with them after a few seconds so that only the two of us remained. He could tell I was puzzled.

"Come on Jass," he said, "don't look so surprised. You had it plastered on your face the second you walked in that door. Plus, you made the trip didn't you?"

"I guess so."

"And don't worry about Theresa, either; she's in an entirely different department from us."

"I'm not following?"

Ryan laughed. "You'll catch on, don't worry."

The rest of the evening flew by. I spent another three hours joking around and getting to know my (hopefully) future co-workers. After a few drinks, both Ryan and Theresa offered me a few more pointers for the interview tomorrow, plus more specifics about the actual job. Essentially, it sounded like it would be part boring project work and part creative fun; the position I was applying for was apparently a hybrid of two other jobs.

"They're looking for someone who can write well but also thinks outside the box," Ryan said at one point. "I think the exact phrase I heard was that they're seeking a right brainer who could switch-hit with their left."

I paid close attention to every word, and in particular kept my distance from Theresa (whose comments became more flirtatious with each beer she drank). She referenced my cuteness at least a dozen times and kept slipping in random comments that clearly implied she was single. Still, in another department or not, I wasn't about to make that sort of blunder before I even got hired. So I nursed a second and then a third beer, limiting myself to three because if I went beyond that, I might not say no to Ryan's next weed offer or Theresa's flirty advances.

By the time I left, it was close to midnight. Everyone said goodbye to me in unison and wished me luck tomorrow. I felt proud that, at the very least, I had the staff of Rydel pulling for me to get the job. Having that support helped ease whatever tension still ran through my muscles.

Though it would have made much more sense to take a cab back to the hotel, I couldn't imagine not walking at this point. I had botched the opportunity to visit any well-known tourist attractions, but I could at least revel in the city's nightlife by taking another walk back to the hotel. So I turned left and began to retrace my steps.

In my solitude, I began to think again about Annabelle. I wanted to ask her if I had passed any of the places she encountered during her visit, or if I might stumble upon the same memorabilia she had taken home with her. I thought about the future and how, if I lived here for a while, I'd be able to tell her about the concerts in town, the best place to get an Italian meal, the hottest late-night clubs. She'd be the outsider this time, like I had been in Portland.

When I got back to my hotel, every ounce of fatigue hit me at once. My body collapsed on top of the bed, the feeling of fresh covers nearly sucking me under. I stared up at the empty white-plastered ceiling, realizing that the view in this bed did not differ in the slightest from my room at Tundra, or even at home. Still, I knew I was somewhere *different*. Which was what I had wanted all along, right? And while I was alone in this tiny impersonal hotel room in this huge impersonal city, that fact didn't really bother me. I was on my way somewhere to do something. It would just be a matter of time until I figured all that out. And maybe no time at all, if tomorrow's interview went well.

Finally, before I shut my eyes, I came to the realization that I was not the only person going for an important job interview tomorrow. A few hundred miles away, Carrie was likely rehearsing a script of her career aspirations, or jotting down frequently asked interview questions, or perhaps sleeping soundly against her pillow. I opened my phone and texted her, wishing her good luck. And then, without waiting for her to respond, I sank into a deep dreamless sleep. But it didn't matter. No response came.

I arrived to my interview forty-five minutes early, as Ryan had advised. Apparently Tonberry's primary pet peeve was punctuality, so he advised that I give myself a cushion of extra time. The place was quite a sight. Maybe it's because I was so accustomed to the classic styles of Tundra, but Rydel oozed with modern style and atmosphere. They had everything from ergonomically-correct chairs to scattered snack trays to unique and colorful design patterns on the walls. Even the cubicle spaces were about twice the size of what I'd been expecting, offering a much more comfortable place where people could stretch their legs without fear of kicking their neighbors.

A secretary greeted me and showed me to the interview room. I sat down in the silver metallic chair, the humming sounds of the air conditioner filling an otherwise silent room. My suit coat was a bit wrinkled, and I kicked myself for not thinking to have it professionally pressed. Really, though I hadn't even had the time, so I decided to strategically position myself in the chair so that the wrinkles would be hidden. Unfortunately that didn't last long since the door opened just moments later, and I stood up to greet Tonberry, who I recognized immediately from Ryan and Theresa's descriptions. He stood about four inches taller than me, his face dripping with sweat, his grizzled salt and pepper beard looking like that of an aging mountain man. They were right; he was indeed a hard-ass.

I held my resume, notepads and pen in one hand and shook his hand with the other.

"Please," he said, pointing to the chair where I had been sitting, "have a seat."

Once the interview wrapped up and I stopped by Ryan's cubicle to say good-bye one more time, I left the office. Immediately, I began to reflect on every word of our exchange. I'd like to believe my preparation had paid off;

that my extensive research helped spark some improvisational skills that I had never possessed before. Ryan and Theresa's warnings were grounded; Tonberry did throw a few hardballs my way, like 'if you caught someone cheating on a test, would you turn them in,' or 'how many hours of overtime should a person be expected to work in a given week' to name a few, but I think I countered those well by answering them honestly ('no, he's only hurting himself') and directly ('any amount necessary').

Still, perception didn't constitute reality, and it's quite possible Tonberry walked out thinking I was some cocky, naïve kid who was in way over his head. I had no way of knowing, and I'd exhausted my communication with Ryan, at least for the time being.

Shortly after I checked out of the hotel, I called Greg and told him about my night at the party and the interview. He was hesitantly enthusiastic, which I interpreted as his official blessing, and my assumption was further bolstered by the fact that when my bus arrived back home, Greg was right there to pick me up and take me back to campus.

The last week of senior year was a breeze. I coasted from one class to another with little to get in the way of my good time. Acing a test took a backseat to nailing a job interview, and while I awaited word from Rydel (good or bad), I started reaching out to other prospects and submitting my resume to interesting-looking job openings, all in New York City. I finally accepted the fact that even if Rydel fell through, I needed to go back. Still, I performed well on my final exams, a testimony to my natural skills as a test taker. I was headed straight for a 3.75 GPA, which was on par with all the other semesters.

In the end though, neither the exams nor the GPA mattered. Tonberry called me the day before my very last exam to congratulate me and offer me the position at Rydel. Shortly after I found an email from Ryan, who told me to keep my phone on. I looked at the timestamp: it was about fifteen minutes before I had gotten the call from Tonberry. To keep with our tradition of short emails, all I wrote back was:

*See you soon on the Upper East Side.*

Coincidentally, Greg's internship officially morphed into a full-time job opportunity just a day after I received word about the position at Rydel, and both of us were set to start working two weeks after graduation. The night before our graduation ceremony, Greg purchased us a bottle of champagne, and we toasted each other while we imagined our new lives. Suddenly, the 'what if' had turned into 'what's next'.

During Tundra's graduation ceremony, I tried my best listening to the keynote speaker's rambling speech—which should have been way more interesting given that he was supposed to be some sort of medical genius—but my mind kept drifting elsewhere. To me, the days of listening to long lecturers were over; it was time to go out and engage with people, to talk and listen, and hear and be heard. I remained in a fog-like jade the entire time, sitting patiently until the celebratory part of the ceremony arrived, where my name was announced and I took the stage to claim my degree.

I knew my parents sat somewhere in the audience watching me during that moment but I chose not to try and find them among the crowd. The feud with my father had never officially settled; it just sort of drifted away to that unknown abyss of forgotten arguments that I sometimes tend to have with friends and family. My father was an overly stubborn person but, I'd like to believe that when I finally buckled down and told him about Rydel, there was at least a small part of fatherly pride surfacing somewhere. And so while I can't recall him every saying the word 'congratulations' per se, I took his apathetic attitude as a sign of forgiveness. And like a typical mother, mine chose to avoid any formal acknowledgment of my leaving, at least during the few moments we shared together. At one point, when I told her that being in New York City was just like being away at Tundra, I could tell she was holding back tears, because she only smiled and told me how nice I looked in my cap and gown.

The second the Dean finished his closing remarks, a good chunk of my classmates bolted out the doors with their families, toward the parking lot. I could understand their hurry; with only a couple hundred yards separating you from the rest of your life, rushing made sense to most people. I, on the other hand took my time; for the next two weeks, I wanted to eliminate any sense of urgency from my life. I had experienced enough of that this month, and there was a lifetime of stress awaiting me in New York. Still, my mother and father were clearly impatient, my father tapping the face of his watch as he approached me.

"Time to hit the road son," my father said. "Want to beat that Saturday night traffic."

"How about we pick up some lobster and maybe a bottle of wine to celebrate tonight?" my mom chimed in.

"Maybe," I responded, my eyes still glued to the fifty or so students still lingering within the assembly hall. "Why don't you guys go ahead, and I'll meet up with you later."

"And how will you get home?" my mom asked.

"Oh I'll find a way," I responded. "Somehow I always do."

"Let him enjoy himself, Evie," my dad said, still watching the cars as the traffic continued to back up further into campus. "Our son's a grown man, now." His comment may have been sarcastic, but I didn't question his approval. I gave them each a hug, assuring them I'd see them later, and took off toward the other end of the auditorium. Everyone still wore their caps and gowns, so from afar we probably all looked identical. But still, though I couldn't pinpoint what made her stand out, my eyes were drawn to

Carrie almost immediately. She leaned against the wall near the back of the room, empty-handed (I imagined her diploma was already framed and stored in a safe somewhere) and laughing.

I hadn't spoken to Carrie in person since that night in her dorm. We were forced to encounter each other every now and then during the last week of classes, and while I had always wanted to approach her, the fear of pissing her off even further kept me at bay. Instead, I had forced Greg (who remained in her good graces) to keep me apprised of what was happening with her. But now, knowing that the only chances of mending any bond with her would be gone after tonight, I made the move.

To get to Carrie, I had to bypass Stacey, who was standing right next to her. She glared at me as I approached, but said nothing.

"Congrats graduates," I murmured. I knew I didn't deserve to be so candid and informal with either girl—especially Carrie—but it felt unnatural to behave any other way.

"You too, graduate," Carrie responded. "I heard about New York."

"And I heard about Pitt Med." Greg had told me she had officially got hired last week. "Not that there was a doubt in either of our minds."

She paused for a moment, turning to look meaningfully at Stacey. Stacey took the hint and stepped away, picking up a conversation with another fellow graduate. Carrie turned back to me.

"I'm really happy for you, Jass."

Her sincerity nearly made me drop my diploma. She didn't hate me.

"Thanks Carrie. Go save some lives. And don't be a stranger, ok?"

I leaned forward and hugged her, any hesitation wiped away when she embraced me right back. We held on to each other for a few seconds. I squeezed even tighter, making up for the fact that I had never hugged her goodbye the night we broke up. I poured everything into that squeeze, all the love, all the regret. She let go first and smiled one more time. A million words, thoughts and phrases formed in my head, and I could have uttered any one of them, but I knew that none would adequately express what I felt. So instead I turned to walk away. I had only taken a few steps when she called my name.

"Jass?"

"Yeah?"

"Save a spot for me in New York City, ok? The day might come when I get brave like you and take a leap."

"There'll always be a spot, Carrie."

I left again, knowing that Carrie wouldn't stop me this time. Across the room, I spotted Greg with a few other friends. He had obviously watched my exchange with Carrie, because he was staring right at me with a huge grin on his face.

"We did it, Jass."

I nodded. "Hard to believe. Are you ready to close up shop?"

"Last party at Millers, if you're coming. I hope you left room for a few more campus memories before you desert us all."

"You guys go ahead, I'll catch up." I didn't hug Greg like I had Carrie, knowing there'd be a few drinks in me soon and there would be plenty of hugging to do. The fresh Tundra alumni were eager to throw the party of their lifetimes, drinking and spouting the millions of great memories that had formed over the past four years: the mistaken hookups, the cram sessions, the drunk dials.

But everything that I had experienced was forever secured in my mind; I didn't need a formal sendoff. Instead, I detoured to the path that led to the football field. The field was empty, the grass slightly moist from an earlier rain and quiet enough that I could hear my feet squishing with every step.

As I walked across the field, the bleachers and scoreboard in front of me became hazy, and images of Konacks flickered through my mind. I extended my right hand, as if Annabelle were standing next to me, ready to take it. My hand touched nothing but air, but at that very moment I felt her presence there on the field. I pictured her on that blanket, right in the moment when she made me swear that I wouldn't accept everything I had coming without putting up a fight.

I'd like to think I kept that promise.

****

Dear readers,

Writing this entry wasn't easy. In fact, for twenty minutes I stared at a white screen, unable to actually type the words that I knew I needed to say—both to all of you, and to myself. I suppose I always knew this day would come, but my only hope from the beginning was that it would be on my terms. Thankfully it has, as a consistent and growing readership (combined with my miraculous ability to find interesting things to write about on a regular basis) has prevented my blog from withering away into obscurity, as so many others tend to do.

A little while ago, I was fortunate enough to be granted an interview with the Arts & Entertainment editor at Culture Guru, a New York-based magazine I've subscribed to and admired for over a decade. Three weeks, four interviews, and a plane ride later, said editor called my cell phone to personally inform me that I've been hired as a writer, and will be producing a weekly column on music, theater, and other artistic happenings around the city. The best part?

The editor found me after being referred to my blog by two members of his staff. Apparently my readership extends all the way to the east coast!

During the interviews, I (reasonably) assumed that my concert reviews, album critiques, and overall artistic endeavors were the source of his interest. Why else would the A&E editor (or his co-workers, for that matter) take any interest in me, let alone trust me with such a huge undertaking? So imagine my surprise when, midway through the interview, he blurted out the question: "So has Jasper called you yet?" No hyperbole: I almost fell out of my chair. "Jasper?" I laughed it off, trying to remain cool (it was still a job interview, after all), but it was then that I realized my blog had totally transformed without my even realizing it. Those five posts about the mysterious college boy I met one night at a concert created an opening into my life that I had never intended and, in some ways, offered more insight into me as a writer—and as an person—than any other writing I've ever done. Still, when Culture Guru officially hired me (I start next Monday!), I came to a crossroads. What should I do about this blog?

With my writing appearing in print (and online under the banner of an official publication—check me out at cultureguru.com!), I think it's time for the Miss Mezzanine blog to come to its natural conclusion. It began as a Portland arts and culture blog, and that's what it shall remain to the end. And end it must, because I will no longer be in Portland to write about all the awesome happenings here! I only hope that you, my readers—who have been my inspiration and motivation throughout this fantastic journey—will continue to read my new column. In return, I promise you the same dedication from me you've come to expect. I'll still be covering the same types of stories, except this time when I review a new album, some poor intern will be fetching a demo copy, and I won't have to dish out fifteen bucks to buy it.

But before I close the door on this chapter of my life, and even though I expect you'll never read this, I must thank you, Jasper. Since that night at the concert, something in my life changed, and it's made its way through everything I've written on this site, infusing even those stories that had nothing to do with you. And while we shared only one night together, the universe has taught me that connections we make can be separated but never broken.

Therefore, Jasper, I leave you this last entry, in case one day, through whatever serendipitous means, you come across these writings. By that time, we may both be in entirely different stages of our life: living in luxury, married to the loves of our lives, raising beautiful children. But like the greatest of songs, the music we created that night will remain engraved in our minds forever, with us wherever we go. And the next time I walk through the woods at night, or lay on a blanket in a grassy field, I'll remember that night, and listen to the sounds of that song play through my head with full clarity and reverence. And I hope one day you'll listen with me.

With love,

Annabelle

# ACKNOWLEDGEMENTS

This story's journey from concept to print carries a significant number of influences, without whom this book could not be possible. To Justin Pastrick, I thank you for using your artistic talents and transforming Miss Mezzanine into a striking cover image. To Zaire Lewis for dealing with my multiple screw-ups as we recorded the audio together. To Mike Guzzi for your eagle eyes, and for being the final gatekeeper between my words and the world.

A big thank you to my beta readers who helped me out so early in the process. To Holly Dynoske for never shying away from your honest thoughts and constantly coaching me along the way. To Rami Bensasi for sharing your insights, which I'll remember when you one day become famous in your own right. To Armand Ventura for reading every piece of my writing since we were kids, and continuing to inspire me with your artistic capabilities. To Amadeo Fusca, for demonstrating your niche in storytelling and passing along some much-needed criticism of the book's early draft. To Alexa Casciato, for bringing the book to life through voice, and for ensuring that my Portland setting was authentic and true to the city's wonderful attributes. I'm thrilled we could team up on another project together, and I'm sure this book will be just a speckle within your future successes as an artist.

Thank you to my family, to my mother and father, for instilling in me discipline, responsibility and hard-work, all characteristics you possess, which I've tried my best to replicate during the completion of this book. To my wife Gabrielle, I thank for not only tolerating my endless nights typing away on Jass's story but for encouraging me never to stop. Amidst every draft, every rewrite, every frustrating hour I worked on this novel, you stood behind me, providing every ounce of support possible. You are a rare gem, and I thank my lucky stars every day that I can call you my wife.

And finally, to my editor and friend, Allison Goldstein, for holding me to a higher standard than I probably deserved. You've pushed me harder than anyone else ever has, and for that I am eternally grateful. Every edit, every comment, every note resonated with me, which not only enhanced this book's final content, but provided further evidence of your amazing capabilities as a writer and editor. Your talents are rare and your honest yet collaborative approach to working with writers is a testament to your future in this industry.

Made in the USA
Charleston, SC
30 January 2014